D1527963

The Sagging Situation

Killian Flinn

The Sagging Situation Killian Flinn
Publisher: Killian Flinn
Publication Date: December 2024
Edition: First Edition

Table of Contents:

brings.

Chapter 3: The Frustration
Kenneth grapples with how his style impacts others' perceptions.

Chapter 4: The Decision
A pivotal choice changes Kenneth's path.

Chapter 5: The Arrest
A turning point that forces Kenneth to confront his reality.

Chapter 6: The Warning
The meaning of sagging pants in prison and its implications.

Chapter 7: The Disbelief
Kenneth's struggle to accept hard truths.

Chapter 8: The Encounter
A moment that reshapes Kenneth's understanding of respect and self-image.

Chapter 9: The Ambush

An event that pushes Kenneth to the brink, with lasting consequences.

Chapter 10: The Aftermath
Recovering from trauma and reevaluating his choices.

Chapter 11: The Realization
Kenneth begins to see the deeper issues behind his decisions.

Chapter 12: The Lesson
A mentor's advice sets Kenneth on a new course.

Chapter 13: The Transformation
Kenneth starts to rebuild himself and his life.

Chapter 14: The Preparation
Preparing for life after prison, armed with newfound wisdom.

Chapter 15: The Freedom
Kenneth is released and faces the

challenges of reintegration.

Chapter 16: The Job
Hard work becomes a foundation for Kenneth's new life.

Chapter 17: The Family
Reconnecting with Carla and creating a strong family bond.

Chapter 18: The Release
Kenneth begins to live his second chance with purpose.

Chapter 19: The Reflection
Looking back on the journey and lessons learned.

Chapter 20: The New Beginning
A fresh start grounded in hope and hard work.

Chapter 21: The Sagging Situation
Kenneth's reflection on the significance of his past choices.

Chapter 22: The Impact
Kenneth's mentorship and the influence of his story on others.

Chapter 23: The Message
Sharing his experiences and inspiring a new generation.

Chapter 24: The Hope
Teaching his sons the value of hope and perseverance.

Chapter 25: A New Dawn
A heartfelt conclusion, focused on legacy and growth.

Chapter 1: The Idol

Kenneth Gilbert was only 18 years old, but he had already experienced more than his fair share of struggles. Growing up in a low-income household with a single mother working multiple jobs to make ends meet, Kenneth had learned to rely on himself from a young age. Despite the challenges, he had always been a bright and curious kid, with a passion for music and a love for hip-hop.

As he navigated the halls of his high school, Kenneth couldn't help but feel like an outsider. His style was different, his interests were different, and his attitude was different. While his classmates were content with blending in with the crowd, Kenneth yearned to stand out.

One day, while browsing through social media, Kenneth stumbled upon a video of his favorite rapper, Vicious V. The rapper's confidence, charisma, and unapologetic swagger resonated deeply with Kenneth. He felt seen, he felt heard, and he felt inspired.

From that moment on, Kenneth became obsessed with Vicious V. He spent hours upon hours studying the rapper's lyrics, watching his interviews, and analyzing his music videos. He even went as far as to mimic the rapper's style, donning baggy jeans, oversized t-shirts, and a fresh new pair of Savage Sneaks.

Kenneth's friends and family noticed the change in him, but they didn't quite understand it. "Why are you dressing like that?" his mother would ask, shaking her head in dismay. "You're not a rapper, Kenneth. You're a high school student."

But Kenneth didn't care. For the first time in his life, he felt like he had found someone who truly understood him. Someone who shared his passions, his interests, and his attitude. Vicious V had become Kenneth's idol, and he was determined to emulate him in every way possible.

Little did Kenneth know, his obsession with Vicious V would soon lead him down a path of self-discovery, a path that would challenge everything he thought he knew about himself.

As Kenneth walked through the halls of his high school, he couldn't help but feel a sense of pride and confidence. He was finally expressing himself, finally being true to who he was. But as he turned a corner, he caught the eye of a classmate, a boy who seemed to be staring right through him.

"Hey, Kenneth," the boy said, his voice low and smooth. "I've seen you around. You're quite the fan of Vicious V, huh?"

Kenneth felt a surge of excitement, a sense of validation. Someone had finally noticed him, finally understood him.

"Yeah, man," Kenneth replied, trying to sound cool. "He's my idol. I love his music, his style, everything."

The boy smiled, his eyes glinting with amusement. "I can see that," he said. "You're definitely... expressive."
Kenneth felt a sense of unease, a sense of uncertainty. What did the boy mean by "expressive"? Was it a compliment, or was it something more?
As he stood there, frozen in uncertainty, the boy took a step closer, his eyes locked onto Kenneth's.
"My name is E-Money," the boy said, his voice low and smooth. "And you are...?"
Kenneth's heart skipped a beat as he replied, his voice barely above a whisper.
"I'm Kenneth." ...as he stood there, frozen in uncertainty, E-Money took another step closer, his eyes never leaving Kenneth's.
"So, Kenneth, what do you think about Vicious V's latest album?" E-Money asked, his voice low and smooth.
Kenneth's mind went blank as he tried to think of a response. He had listened to the album countless times, but he couldn't think of anything to say.
"It's... it's okay, I guess," Kenneth stuttered, feeling his face heat up with embarrassment.
E-Money chuckled, his eyes glinting with amusement. "Just okay? Vicious V is a genius, man. His lyrics are deep, his flow is sick, and his style is on point."
Kenneth felt a surge of defensiveness, but E-Money's words were laced with a sincerity that made Kenneth want to listen.
"I know, right?" Kenneth said, trying to sound cool. "I love his music, but sometimes I feel like he's just repeating himself."
E-Money's expression turned serious, his eyes narrowing slightly. "You think Vicious V is repetitive? Man, you must not be listening to his music right."
Kenneth felt a pang of uncertainty, wondering if he had misinterpreted Vicious V's music.
"I don't know, maybe I'm just not getting it," Kenneth said, feeling a sense of vulnerability wash over him.
E-Money smiled, his eyes glinting with amusement. "Don't worry, Kenneth, I'm here to school you on Vicious V's

greatness. Let's grab some lunch and discuss the finer points of his music."

Kenneth's heart skipped a beat as he considered E-Money's offer. He had never really talked to E-Money before, but there was something about him that made Kenneth want to open up.

"Sure, why not?" Kenneth said, trying to sound casual.

As they walked to the cafeteria, E-Money launched into a passionate explanation of Vicious V's lyrics, his words painting a vivid picture of the rapper's genius. Kenneth listened, entranced, feeling like he was seeing Vicious V's music in a whole new light.

But as they sat down at a table, E-Money's expression turned serious, his eyes locking onto Kenneth's.

"Kenneth, can I ask you something?" E-Money said, his voice low and smooth.

Kenneth felt a sense of trepidation, wondering what E-Money was going to ask.

"Sure, what is it?" Kenneth replied, trying to sound calm.

E-Money leaned in, his eyes glinting with a mischievous spark.

"Do you think Vicious V is sexy?" E-Money asked, his voice barely above a whisper.

Kenneth's heart skipped a beat as he considered E-Money's question. He had never really thought about Vicious V in a sexual way before, but now that E-Money mentioned it, he couldn't help but feel a spark of attraction.

"I... I don't know," Kenneth stuttered, feeling his face heat up with embarrassment.

E-Money chuckled, his eyes glinting with amusement.

"Don't worry, Kenneth, your secret is safe with me," E-Money said, his voice low and smooth. "But let's just say, Vicious V is definitely sexy. And I think you might be too."

Kenneth's heart racing, he felt a sense of uncertainty wash over him. What did E-Money mean by that? And why was he feeling this strange, fluttery sensation in his chest?

Kenneth sat there, trying to process E-Money's words, he couldn't help but feel a sense of confusion. What did E-Money mean by saying that Kenneth might be sexy too? And why was he feeling this strange, fluttery sensation in his chest? E-Money seemed to sense Kenneth's confusion, and he leaned in closer, his eyes glinting with amusement.

"Hey, don't worry about it, Kenneth," E-Money said, his voice low and smooth. "I'm just messing with you. But seriously, you're a cool dude, and I'm glad we're hanging out."

Kenneth felt a sense of relief wash over him, and he smiled, trying to play it cool.

"Yeah, no problem, E-Money," Kenneth said, trying to sound casual. "I'm glad we're hanging out too."

As they finished their lunch and headed back to class, Kenneth couldn't help but feel a sense of excitement. He had never really talked to E-Money before, but now he was starting to feel like they might actually become friends.

And as they walked down the hallway, E-Money turned to Kenneth and said, "Hey, man, want to come over to my place after school? My mom's not home, and we can chill and listen to some music."

Kenneth's heart skipped a beat as he considered E-Money's invitation. He had never been to E-Money's house before, and he wasn't sure if he should go.

But as he looked into E-Money's eyes, he saw something there that made him feel like he could trust him.

"Yeah, sure, E-Money," Kenneth said, trying to sound cool. "I'll come over after school."

E-Money grinned, his eyes glinting with excitement.

"Awesome, man," E-Money said, his voice low and smooth. "I'll see you then."

And with that, Kenneth and E-Money parted ways, each of them heading to their next class.

But as Kenneth sat in class, he couldn't help but feel a sense of anticipation. What would happen when he went to E-Money's house after school? And what did E-Money mean by saying that Kenneth might be sexy too?

Kenneth's mind was filled with questions, but one thing was for sure: he was excited to find out.

Chapter 2: The Attention

Kenneth adjusted the waist of his jeans as he strolled through the crowded school hallway, the sagging fabric swaying slightly with every step. His steps were deliberate, casual, just like he had seen Vicious V do in music videos. He felt the eyes on him—some admiring, some scrutinizing—but none of them felt like the validation he had imagined.

“Yo, Ken, loving that vibe, man!” a voice called out. It was one of his classmates, Malik, who gave him an exaggerated nod of approval. Kenneth nodded back with a small smirk. Moments like this felt good, like he was carving out his place in the school’s social landscape.

But as he passed a group of guys lingering by the lockers, the mood shifted.

“Looking good today, Kenny,” one of them drawled, his tone dripping with playful mockery.

“Yeah, real good,” another chimed in, punctuated with a sharp whistle.

Kenneth stiffened, his hand instinctively pulling his jeans higher on his hips. Heat rose to his face as he walked faster, the sound of their laughter following him down the hallway.

He ducked into a bathroom to catch his breath, gripping the edge of the sink as he stared at his reflection. His style was on point: the oversized graphic tee, the chain glinting in the fluorescent light, the perfect slouch to his jeans. So why did it feel so wrong now?

At lunch, Kenneth slid into his usual spot in the corner of the cafeteria, where the noise of the crowd was just background static. He dug into his food, but his mind kept replaying the comments and whistles from earlier.

"Hey, Kenny," E-Money said, appearing seemingly out of nowhere and plopping down across from him. "You good? You look like you're in a whole other universe right now."

Kenneth forced a shrug. "I'm fine, man. Just... some people don't know how to keep their mouths shut."

E-Money smirked knowingly. "Ah, they talking about your sagging game?"

Kenneth scowled. "I don't care what they think."

"Sure you don't." E-Money leaned back, crossing his arms. "Listen, people notice when you stand out. Good, bad, whatever—it means you're doing something right."

Kenneth glanced at E-Money, unsure how to respond. Was this supposed to make him feel better? He appreciated the sentiment, but it wasn't just about standing out. It was about feeling like he was the punchline to a joke he didn't understand.

In the afternoon, things got worse. As Kenneth walked to his final class, he passed by a group of guys lounging near the water fountains. The moment he turned the corner, he could feel their eyes on him.

"Damn, Kenneth, save some for the rest of us!" one of them called out, followed by laughter.

"Y'all wild," another voice said, barely containing his amusement. "Man's out here looking like a snack."

Kenneth's grip tightened on the strap of his backpack. He kept walking, his ears burning, the laughter still echoing behind him. His free hand tugged at his waistband again, but no matter how high he pulled the jeans, it didn't feel like enough.

By the time he reached his classroom, Kenneth felt like his confidence had been stripped away. He dropped into his seat, avoiding eye contact with anyone, and let his hood fall over his head. He had spent so much energy trying to express himself, to stand out, and now it felt like it was all backfiring.

That evening, Kenneth lay on his bed, scrolling through his phone. Videos of Vicious V played on loop, each one showing the rapper effortlessly commanding attention with his style, his confidence, his swagger. Kenneth tried to reconcile that image with the reality he was living. Why was it so easy for Vicious V and so complicated for him?

His mother's voice interrupted his thoughts. "Kenneth, dinner's ready!"

"Not hungry!" he called back, letting the phone fall onto his chest. His thoughts churned, blending frustration with self-doubt. Maybe his mom was right. Maybe he wasn't cut out for this. Or maybe he was just overthinking it. Either way, he knew one thing for sure—he was tired of being the center of attention for the wrong reasons.

As he drifted off to sleep, Kenneth resolved to figure it out. To understand why he felt so uncomfortable in his own skin and what it would take to make things better.

The next day, as he walked into school, Kenneth kept his chin up and his steps steady. He still wore his sagging jeans and oversized tee, but he adjusted his walk—less swagger, more purpose. Maybe today would be different.

"Hey, Kenny," someone called out from the lockers. He

tensed, expecting the worst. Instead, it was E-Money, giving him a casual wave.

Kenneth exhaled, offering a faint smile. Maybe he didn't have everything figured out yet, but he wasn't going to let anyone knock him down. Not today.

Chapter 3: The Frustration

The bell rang, signaling the end of another grueling day at school. Kenneth slung his backpack over one shoulder, pulling his jeans up slightly as he merged into the river of students flowing through the hallways. Each step felt heavier than the last, the day's events weighing on him.

He passed by a group of athletes by the lockers, their laughter erupting as he walked by. One of them cupped his hands around his mouth and yelled, "Looking good, Kenny!" The comment was followed by a whistle that made Kenneth's stomach churn. He clenched his jaw, refusing to turn around, but the heat rising in his cheeks betrayed his frustration.

At home, Kenneth burst through the front door and tossed his backpack onto the couch. His mother, Carla, stood in the kitchen, stirring a pot on the stove. She looked up briefly and noticed his tight-lipped expression.

"What's wrong with you?" she asked, wiping her hands on a dish towel.

"Nothing," Kenneth muttered, heading toward his room.

"Hold on now," Carla said, stepping into the living room. "You're not just going to stomp in here like that without telling me what's going on."

Kenneth stopped, his shoulders tense. He turned around slowly, his eyes avoiding hers. “It’s just school. People don’t know how to mind their business.”

Carla’s expression softened as she crossed her arms. “What kind of business are we talking about?”

Kenneth hesitated. How could he explain the looks, the comments, the whistles? How could he put into words the frustration of feeling both visible and invisible at the same time?

“It’s... nothing, Ma. Just people talking stupid,” he finally said.

Carla sighed. “Listen, I know you’re trying to do your own thing, but you’ve got to think about how you present yourself. People are always going to judge you, especially out there.”

Kenneth’s frustration boiled over. “Why does it matter what I wear? Why can’t people just leave me alone?”

Carla’s gaze softened, and she walked over to him, placing a hand on his shoulder. “You’re right—it shouldn’t matter. But sometimes it does. And you’ve got to be ready for that.”

That night, Kenneth sat on the edge of his bed, scrolling through his social media feed. Pictures of Vicious V filled his screen—on stage, in interviews, posing in his signature sagging jeans and oversized jackets. The rapper looked untouchable, his confidence radiating from every post.

Kenneth set the phone down and stared at the floor. He wanted to feel that kind of confidence, to walk through life without caring what anyone thought. But no matter how hard he tried, the comments and stares chipped away at him, leaving him questioning everything.

The next morning, Kenneth walked into school with a new resolve. He wasn't going to let anyone get to him today. He adjusted his sagging jeans, threw on his favorite hoodie, and kept his chin up as he entered the building.

But it didn't take long for the day to unravel. During second period, a crumpled piece of paper landed on his desk. He opened it cautiously, his heart sinking as he read the message scrawled inside: "Nice butt, Kenny. Too bad you're wasting it on sagging."

Laughter erupted from the back of the room, and Kenneth's face burned with anger. He crumpled the paper and stuffed it into his backpack, avoiding eye contact with the others.

At lunch, the comments continued. He could hear the whispers as he passed by tables, the occasional chuckle or exaggerated whistle. Every noise felt like a spotlight shining on him, highlighting his every move.

E-Money slid into the seat across from him, his tray loaded with fries and a burger. "Yo, Kenny, you good?" he asked, popping a fry into his mouth.

Kenneth stared at his food, his appetite long gone. "Why can't people just leave me alone?" he muttered.

E-Money raised an eyebrow. "What happened?"

Kenneth sighed. "Same stuff. Comments, jokes, people acting like clowns."

E-Money leaned forward, his expression serious. "Listen, man. People are always gonna hate on what they don't understand. You've got a vibe, and they're either jealous or too dumb to get it."

Kenneth shook his head. “It doesn’t feel like that. It feels like I’m just a joke to them.”

“Then stop caring what they think,” E-Money said, his tone firm. “You’re doing you. That’s all that matters.”

Kenneth wanted to believe him, but the knot of frustration in his chest wouldn’t budge.

By the end of the day, Kenneth was ready to snap. As he walked down the hallway toward the exit, he felt someone grab the back of his jeans and yank them up. He spun around, his fists clenched, to see one of the athletes smirking at him.

“Thought I’d help you out, Kenny,” the guy said, his voice dripping with mockery.

Kenneth shoved him back, his voice shaking with anger. “Don’t touch me!”

The hallway went silent as everyone turned to watch. The athlete held up his hands, his grin widening. “Relax, man. Just having some fun.”

Kenneth didn’t respond. He stormed out of the building, his hands trembling as he fought to keep his composure.

That evening, Kenneth sat on the porch steps, staring out at the street. The sun was setting, casting long shadows across the pavement. He replayed the day’s events in his mind, each comment and laugh echoing louder than the last.

He clenched his fists, his frustration bubbling over. He didn’t want to feel like this anymore—angry, self-conscious, trapped. Something had to change, but he didn’t know where to start.

As the streetlights flickered on, Kenneth made a silent promise to himself. He wouldn't let anyone else dictate how he felt about himself. He was tired of feeling small, tired of being a target. Tomorrow, he would take the first step toward reclaiming his confidence.

Whatever that step might be.

Chapter 4: The Decision

Kenneth stood in front of his mirror, staring at his reflection. His jeans hung low on his hips, the baggy fabric bunching over his sneakers. His hoodie draped loosely over his frame, the hood pulled up to obscure most of his face. He tugged at the waistband of his jeans, pulling them slightly higher, but they slid back into place the moment he let go.

His jaw tightened. He hated how something so small could feel so monumental. Adjusting his pants, fixing his hood—it felt like he was patching together a version of himself that didn't quite fit. Yet he couldn't let it go. The comments, the whistles, the laughter—it all echoed in his mind, each word twisting like a knife in his gut. No matter how many times he told himself to brush it off, it lingered.

The mirror offered no answers, only his own tired reflection. His sagging style, once a symbol of freedom, now felt like a magnet for unwanted attention. Still, he couldn't bring himself to abandon it. Vicious V didn't flinch under pressure, and neither would he. Or at least, that's what he told himself.

At school, the hallways buzzed with their usual chaotic energy. Kenneth wove through the throng of students, keeping his head low. He hadn't slept well, and the noise felt sharper, louder today. Each voice seemed to cut through his thoughts, unrelenting.

"Yo, Kenny!" a familiar voice called out. He glanced over to see Malik jogging toward him, his grin as wide as ever. Malik was one of the few people Kenneth could tolerate lately. While others teased or joked at his expense, Malik always seemed genuine.

"Sup, man?" Kenneth said, his tone flat despite the effort to sound normal.

"You good?" Malik asked, slapping a hand on Kenneth's shoulder. "Heard about what happened yesterday."

Kenneth shrugged, his eyes darting toward a group of students leaning against the lockers. "It's whatever."

Malik frowned. "Man, people are dumb. You know that, right? They just see you doing your thing and can't stand it."

Kenneth tried to appreciate Malik's words, but they felt hollow. He nodded half-heartedly. "Yeah, maybe."

"Come on, Kenny," Malik said, his tone softening. "You've got a vibe, man. Own it. Stop letting these clowns mess with your head."

Kenneth forced a small smile, but deep down, he wondered if Malik even understood. How could he own something that felt like it was owning him?

Lunchtime didn't offer much relief. Kenneth sat alone in the corner of the cafeteria, picking at his food. The din of the room swirled around him, the laughter and chatter blending into a steady hum of background noise. Across the room, E-Money sat surrounded by his usual crew, laughing and gesturing animatedly.

Kenneth's gaze lingered on E-Money for a moment. The guy

had it figured out—or at least, he made it look like he did. How did he move through the same hallways, face the same people, and still exude that unshakable confidence? Kenneth wished he could bottle even an ounce of that and carry it with him.

“Hey, Kenny,” a voice interrupted his thoughts. He looked up to see E-Money sliding into the seat across from him, his tray loaded with fries and a burger.

“What’s up?” Kenneth asked, though his tone carried little energy.

E-Money studied him for a moment, his usual grin replaced by something more serious. “You’ve been real quiet lately. That’s not like you.”

Kenneth shrugged, poking at the limp fries on his plate. “Just got a lot on my mind.”

“Let me guess,” E-Money said, leaning forward. “People talking trash? Messing with you?”

Kenneth didn’t respond, but the look in his eyes was enough.

“Man, forget them,” E-Money said, his voice firm. “You’re better than that. Don’t let their noise mess with your head. They’re just jealous.”

“Jealous of what?” Kenneth asked, the bitterness in his voice surprising even himself. “Of getting clowned every time I walk down the hallway?”

“Nah, man. They’re jealous ‘cause you’re doing something different. You’re not scared to be you.”

Kenneth wanted to believe him, but the knot of frustration in his chest wouldn't budge. "It doesn't feel like that," he muttered.

E-Money leaned back in his seat, studying Kenneth for a moment. "You ever think maybe they're just scared of what they don't get? You're out here being yourself, and they don't know how to handle it."

Kenneth sighed. "Maybe."

The walk home felt longer than usual. Kenneth kept his hood up, his hands jammed into his pockets. The comments and laughter from earlier played on a loop in his head. He didn't want to care, but he couldn't shake the feeling of being watched, judged, picked apart.

When he got home, he found his mom, Carla, in the kitchen. The scent of something warm and savory filled the air, but Kenneth barely noticed.

"Hey, baby," Carla said, glancing up from the stove. "You okay? You look tired."

Kenneth shrugged. "Just a long day."

Carla set down the spoon she was holding and walked over to him. "What's going on? You've been coming home like this a lot lately."

"It's nothing," Kenneth said, avoiding her gaze. "Just school stuff."

Carla tilted her head, her eyes narrowing slightly. "You know you can talk to me, right? You don't have to keep everything bottled up."

Kenneth hesitated. How could he explain what he was

feeling? The constant tension, the way every comment chipped away at his confidence? "It's just... people always got something to say," he finally said. "No matter what I do, it's like I can't win."

Carla's expression softened. She placed a hand on his shoulder, her voice gentle. "Baby, people are always gonna have opinions. You can't change that. But you can change how much you let them matter."

Kenneth looked at her, his throat tightening. "It's just hard, Ma. Feels like I can't even be myself without someone turning it into a joke."

Carla nodded, her grip on his shoulder firm. "It's not easy, I know. But you've got to remember who you are. The world doesn't get to tell you that—you do."

Kenneth swallowed hard, her words settling deep in his chest. "Thanks, Ma."

She smiled and ruffled his hair. "Anytime. Now come eat before the food gets cold."

That night, Kenneth lay on his bed, staring at the ceiling. His mom's words echoed in his mind, blending with Malik's encouragement and E-Money's advice. He couldn't control what people thought or said, but he could control how he responded.

He picked up his phone and opened Instagram. A photo of Vicious V filled the screen, the rapper standing on a stage with his arms raised triumphantly. Kenneth stared at the image, his chest tightening. He wanted that confidence, that power. But how could he find it when he felt so trapped?

As the moonlight streamed through his window, Kenneth sat

up. He couldn't let himself be defined by other people's opinions anymore. He couldn't keep living in fear of their judgments. Tomorrow, he would make a change—not in how he dressed or how he walked, but in how he carried himself.

This was his life, his journey. And it was time to take control.

Chapter 5: The Arrest

The afternoon sun hung low, casting long shadows across the storefronts on Kenneth's walk home. He had stopped by the corner store to grab a soda, his earbuds in, blocking out the noise of the bustling street. The day had been exhausting, but he felt lighter than usual. His conversation with his mom replayed in his mind, her words of encouragement anchoring him in a way he hadn't realized he needed.

The bell above the shop's door jingled as Kenneth stepped inside. He nodded at Mr. Patel behind the counter, a familiar face who often greeted him with a smile. Kenneth made his way to the refrigerated section at the back, scanning the shelves for his favorite drink.

"You good, kid?" Mr. Patel asked from the counter, his voice warm.

"Yeah, just grabbing a soda," Kenneth replied, holding up the bottle he'd chosen.

As Kenneth headed to the counter, the door jingled again, and two men entered the store. Kenneth glanced at them briefly, noticing their hushed voices and nervous energy. He didn't think much of it, focusing instead on fishing a few crumpled bills from his pocket.

"Anything else for you?" Mr. Patel asked.

"Nah, just this," Kenneth replied, placing the bottle on the counter.

But before he could hand over the money, a sharp voice cut through the air. "Hands where I can see them!"

Kenneth froze, his heart hammering as he turned to see one of the men pointing something toward the counter. It wasn't a gun—just a hand in his pocket mimicking the shape—but it was enough to make Mr. Patel's face pale.

"Empty the register," the man demanded, his voice trembling with forced authority. His partner stood near the door, glancing nervously at the street outside.

Kenneth took a step back, his hands instinctively raised. "Hey, man, I'm just here for a drink," he said, his voice calm but laced with fear.

"Shut up!" the man snapped, turning toward Kenneth. His glare was fierce, but the sweat on his brow betrayed his panic. "Just stay where you are."

Mr. Patel began fumbling with the register, his hands shaking as he tried to open it. Kenneth stayed rooted to the spot, his mind racing. He wanted to run, to get out of this situation, but his legs wouldn't move.

The second man stepped closer to Kenneth, his voice low but urgent. "You better not do anything stupid."

Kenneth nodded, his throat dry. "I'm not trying to."

The police arrived faster than anyone expected. Red and blue lights flashed outside the store, their glare slicing through the tension inside. The first man cursed under his breath, grabbing a few bills from the register before making a run for the back door. His partner followed, shoving past Kenneth in his haste.

Kenneth barely had time to process what had happened before the door burst open, and two officers stormed in, their guns drawn. “Hands up! Don’t move!” one of them shouted.

“It wasn’t me!” Kenneth blurted, his hands shooting into the air. He stepped back, his heart pounding in his chest. “I didn’t do anything!”

The officers didn’t seem to hear him. One grabbed his arm, twisting it behind his back as the other frisked him roughly. “You think you’re slick, huh?” the officer muttered.

“What? No!” Kenneth protested, wincing as the handcuffs bit into his wrists. “I was just buying a soda!”

“Save it,” the officer snapped, pulling Kenneth toward the door.

Outside, a small crowd had gathered, their murmurs filling the air. Kenneth’s face burned as he saw the judgment in their eyes. A few people held up their phones, recording the scene as the officers pushed him toward the squad car.

“Wait!” Mr. Patel called, stepping out of the store. “You have the wrong person! He didn’t do anything!”

The officers paused, their expressions skeptical. “What do you mean?” one of them asked.

“The boy was just a customer,” Mr. Patel explained, his voice firm. “The real thieves ran out the back. Check your cameras if you don’t believe me.”

Kenneth looked at Mr. Patel, relief and gratitude washing over him. “Thank you,” he managed to say, his voice shaky.

The officers exchanged a glance before one of them sighed and reached for the radio. “We’ve got two suspects fleeing on foot,” he said. “Send backup to the area.”

The other officer removed the cuffs from Kenneth’s wrists, his expression unreadable. “You’re free to go,” he said gruffly, not meeting Kenneth’s eyes.

The walk home was a blur. Kenneth’s wrists ached from the cuffs, and his chest felt tight with a mix of anger and humiliation. He replayed the events in his mind, each moment sharpening his frustration. He hadn’t done anything wrong, yet he had been treated like a criminal. Why? Because he happened to be there? Because he looked a certain way?

When he got home, Carla was waiting for him, her arms crossed and worry etched into her face. “What happened?” she asked, her voice trembling.

Kenneth hesitated, his throat tightening. “I... I got stopped by the cops,” he admitted. “They thought I was part of a robbery.”

Carla’s eyes widened, and she stepped closer, placing her hands on his shoulders. “Are you okay?”

Kenneth nodded, but the words felt hollow. “I’m fine, Ma. They let me go.”

Carla’s expression shifted from fear to anger. “This isn’t right,” she said, her voice firm. “You didn’t deserve that.”

“I know,” Kenneth said quietly. He sat down on the couch, his head in his hands. “I didn’t even do anything.”

Carla sat beside him, her voice softening. “I’m sorry, baby. I’m so sorry you had to go through that."

Kenneth looked at her, his eyes glistening with unshed tears. "Why does this keep happening? Why can't people just see me for me?"

Carla sighed, wrapping an arm around his shoulders. "Sometimes the world's unfair, Kenneth. But you're strong. You don't let it define you, hear me?"

Kenneth nodded, her words sinking into his heart. He wasn't sure how to move forward, but he knew one thing: he couldn't let this break him.

That night, Kenneth lay in bed, staring at the ceiling. The events of the day replayed in his mind, each moment stoking the fire in his chest. He had felt powerless, invisible, reduced to a stereotype. But he didn't want to stay in that place.

As the darkness pressed around him, a spark of determination ignited. He couldn't change how people saw him, but he could change how he responded. He wouldn't let them win. He wouldn't let their assumptions define him.

Tomorrow, he would walk into school with his head held high. He would wear his style like armor, not because it made him invisible, but because it made him feel seen. And no one could take that from him.

Chapter 6: The Warning

The next morning, Kenneth sat at the kitchen table, staring at a bowl of cereal that had long since gone soggy. His appetite was nowhere to be found, his mind tangled in the events of the previous day. The cuffs biting into his wrists, the crowd's judgmental eyes, the humiliation of being dragged out like a criminal—it all replayed in his head on an endless loop.

Carla walked in, carrying her coffee mug. She took one look at Kenneth's expression and set the mug down with a sigh. "You're thinking about yesterday, aren't you?" she asked gently.

Kenneth nodded. "It's hard not to."

Carla pulled out the chair beside him and sat down, her hands wrapping around her mug for warmth. "Baby, what happened to you wasn't fair. It wasn't right. But I need you to understand something—it could've been worse."

Kenneth looked up at her, his brow furrowing. "Worse? I didn't even do anything, and they still treated me like a criminal."

"I know," Carla said, her voice steady. "But you're a young Black man in this world, Kenneth. That means you're going to face things other people don't. You have to stay smart out there, no matter how unfair it feels."

Kenneth's jaw tightened. "So what am I supposed to do? Just let people think whatever they want about me?"

Carla reached out and placed a hand on his. "No. You stand tall, you stay true to yourself, but you keep your head on straight. Don't give them any excuses to make it worse."

Kenneth pulled his hand away, frustration bubbling to the surface. "That's easy for you to say, Ma. You're not the one walking into school every day, dealing with people staring, judging, making comments."

Carla's expression softened. "You're right. I don't know what it's like for you at school. But I do know that you're stronger than this. Don't let them take that from you."

At school, the whispers started as soon as Kenneth stepped through the doors. Word had spread about his encounter with the police, and it didn't take long for the rumors to spiral out of control.

"I heard he got arrested for stealing," someone whispered as he passed.

"Nah, they said he was part of some gang," another voice added.

Kenneth clenched his fists, keeping his eyes forward. He didn't have the energy to confront every lie, but each word cut deeper than he wanted to admit. By the time he reached his locker, he felt like a tightly wound spring, ready to snap at the slightest provocation.

E-Money was waiting for him, leaning against the lockers with his usual nonchalant grin. "Yo, Kenny. You good?"

Kenneth slammed his locker shut, the sound echoing down the hall. "Do I look good to you?" he snapped.

E-Money held up his hands in mock surrender. "Chill, man. I'm just checking in."

Kenneth sighed, rubbing a hand over his face. "Sorry. It's just... everything feels messed up right now."

E-Money nodded, his expression unusually serious. "Yeah, I heard what happened. That's rough, man. You didn't deserve that."

"Tell that to everyone else," Kenneth muttered. "Half the school thinks I'm some kind of thug now."

"Let them think what they want," E-Money said, shrugging.

"You know the truth. That's all that matters."

Kenneth looked at him, frustration still simmering beneath the surface. "That's easy for you to say. You're not the one they're talking about."

E-Money's grin faded, and he leaned in closer. "Listen, man. I get it. People love to run their mouths, especially when they don't know what they're talking about. But you can't let them control you. You gotta keep doing you."

Kenneth wanted to believe him, but it was hard to see past the weight of the day's rumors. "Yeah. Easier said than done."

By lunch, the tension had reached its peak. Kenneth sat at a table by himself, his hood pulled low over his head. He could feel the stares, hear the whispers, and it made his skin crawl. For the first time in a long while, he wished he could just disappear.

Malik slid into the seat across from him, his tray clattering onto the table. "Yo, Kenny. What's good?"

Kenneth didn't look up. "Not much."

Malik frowned, leaning forward. "You gotta stop letting these people get in your head, man. They're just talking to hear themselves talk."

"Yeah, well, it's working," Kenneth muttered. "Feels like I can't even breathe without someone having something to say."

Malik reached over and tapped the edge of Kenneth's tray. "Then make 'em talk about something else. Show them who you really are. Don't let their nonsense define you."

Kenneth finally looked up, his eyes meeting Malik's. "And how am I supposed to do that?"

Malik grinned. "Start by sitting with us. People see you sitting here all quiet, they're gonna keep thinking you're hiding something. Come hang with the crew and remind them who Kenneth really is."

Kenneth hesitated. The idea of facing the cafeteria crowd felt daunting, but he could see the logic in Malik's words. If he wanted to take back control of his narrative, he had to start somewhere.

"Alright," Kenneth said, his voice low but firm. "Let's do it."

The rest of the day passed in a blur. Kenneth kept his head down, trying to focus on his classes and ignore the noise around him. By the time the final bell rang, he felt drained, but a small part of him also felt lighter. He had made it through the day, and that was enough for now.

As he walked home, Carla's words replayed in his mind. "Stay smart. Don't give them any excuses." He didn't like the reality of it, but he knew she was right. The world wasn't fair, and it was up to him to navigate it as best he could.

When he got home, he went straight to his room and grabbed his journal. Writing had always been his outlet, a way to process his thoughts when the world felt too loud. He opened to a blank page and began to write, letting the words flow without overthinking.

Dear Journal,

Today was rough. Feels like the whole school is watching me, waiting for me to mess up. I hate how people can make you feel like you're nothing, like your whole existence is just a joke. But I'm trying. I'm trying to remember what Mom said, what E-

Money and Malik keep telling me.

I can't let them win. I can't let their words define me. I don't know how to fix this yet, but I'm gonna figure it out. One step at a time.

As Kenneth closed the journal, he felt a small sense of relief. He didn't have all the answers, but at least he was trying. And for now, that was enough.

Chapter 7: The Disbelief

Kenneth stood at the edge of the gym, his arms crossed tightly over his chest. The sharp whistle of the coach echoed through the air, signaling the start of another basketball game. Normally, he stayed in the background during gym class, content to watch from the sidelines or half-heartedly jog laps. But today, his stomach churned with unease.

The rumors hadn't just spread—they'd taken on a life of their own. Every hallway he walked down, every glance cast in his direction, felt heavier. Whispers about his "arrest" weren't just misinformed—they'd evolved into something worse. People weren't just questioning what happened; they were questioning him.

"Yo, Kenny!" someone called from the court. Kenneth didn't respond. He kept his arms crossed, his expression neutral, though he felt anything but calm.

"You hear me, Kenny?" The voice came closer now, mocking. "I said, nice fit, man. Still sagging after all that, huh?"

Laughter erupted from a group of boys behind him. Kenneth stiffened, his jaw tightening as his hands clenched into fists. He could feel their eyes on him, examining, judging, making assumptions. It wasn't just about his style anymore. It was about what they thought it said about him.

By the time lunch rolled around, Kenneth had reached his limit. He sat with Malik and a couple of other guys, trying to focus on their conversation, but his mind kept circling back to the gym.

"Yo, Kenny, you okay?" Malik asked, nudging him with an elbow.

Kenneth sighed. "No. I'm not."

"What's up?" Malik leaned in, his tone serious now.

Kenneth hesitated, then spoke. "It's these rumors, man. It's like... it's not just about what happened with the cops anymore. People are looking at me like I'm some kind of joke."

Malik frowned. "What do you mean?"

Kenneth glanced around the cafeteria, lowering his voice. "It's like... I don't know. Guys are acting weird. Saying stuff about my pants, like I'm out here sagging for them or something."

Malik let out a short laugh, but it wasn't mocking—it was more like disbelief. "They're really saying that?"

Kenneth nodded, his frustration bubbling over. "Yeah. Every time I walk down the hall, I hear them whispering. It's not even about the cops anymore. It's like they're... questioning me."

Malik shook his head. "Man, that's wild. But you know what? Forget them. They're just trying to mess with you 'cause they don't get it."

"That's the problem," Kenneth muttered. "They don't get it, but they act like they do. Like they know me. Like they know why I sag my pants."

That afternoon, things came to a head. Kenneth was at his locker, swapping out his books, when a group of guys passed by. He could feel their eyes on him before they even said a word.

"Yo, Kenny!" one of them called. "What's good with those pants, man? Trying to show off for us?"

The laughter that followed sent a jolt of anger through Kenneth's chest. He slammed his locker shut and turned to face them. "What's your problem?" he demanded, his voice sharp.

The leader of the group smirked, crossing his arms. "No problem, man. Just wondering why you're out here showing all that off."

Kenneth's fists clenched at his sides. "I'm not showing off anything. This is how I dress."

"Sure it is," another guy chimed in, his tone dripping with mockery. "But it's a little... extra, don't you think?"

Kenneth took a step forward, his glare icy. "Say what you're trying to say."

The smirk faltered for a moment, but the guy didn't back down. "I'm just saying... maybe you're not as straight as you think."

A wave of heat rushed to Kenneth's face. He wanted to yell, to fight, to shut them up once and for all, but his voice caught in his throat. Before he could respond, a teacher's voice cut through the tension.

"Gentlemen! Is there a problem here?"

The group quickly dispersed, leaving Kenneth standing there, his chest heaving with barely contained anger.

When Kenneth got home, Carla was waiting for him, a concerned look on her face. "Rough day?" she asked as he dropped his bag by the door.

"You could say that," Kenneth muttered, heading for the couch.

Carla followed him, sitting beside him. "Want to talk about it?"

Kenneth hesitated, then shook his head. "It's nothing. Just... people being stupid."

Carla studied him for a moment, her expression softening. "Is this about the rumors?"

Kenneth looked at her, surprised. "You know about that?"

"Of course I do," Carla said. "I'm your mother. People talk, and I hear things. But I didn't think it was still bothering you."

"It's not just the rumors," Kenneth admitted. "It's what they're turning into. It's like... people are looking at me differently now. Like they think they know something about me that's not true."

Carla tilted her head. "And you think it's because of how you dress?"

Kenneth shrugged. "Maybe. I don't know. It feels like everything I do is under a microscope. Like people are just waiting to tear me apart."

Carla placed a hand on his shoulder. "Kenneth, listen to me.

You can't control what other people think. But you can control how much you let it affect you."

Kenneth looked away. "That's easy to say, Ma. But it's not easy to do."

"No, it's not," Carla agreed. "But you're stronger than you think. And if you want people to see you for who you really are, you have to stop letting their opinions define you."

That night, Kenneth sat at his desk, staring at a blank page in his journal. The words didn't come easily, but eventually, he began to write.

Dear Journal,

Today was hard. People keep talking about me, about my pants, about things that don't even make sense. I don't get why they care so much. Why can't they just leave me alone?

I like the way I dress. It makes me feel like me. But now it feels like I'm walking around with a target on my back. I'm not trying to send any messages—I'm just trying to be myself. But maybe that's the problem. Maybe being myself is too much for some people.

I don't know what to do. But I know I can't let them win.

As he closed the journal, Kenneth let out a long breath. He didn't have all the answers, but he knew one thing—he wasn't going to let their whispers break him. Not now, and not ever.

Chapter 8: The Encounter

Kenneth walked through the hallway, his steps steady but his mind turbulent. His sagging jeans swayed slightly with each step, drawing glances that felt sharper than ever. Whispers trailed him like a shadow, and even though he tried to keep his head up, the weight of it all was becoming unbearable.

He turned a corner toward his locker, hoping to grab his things and leave without incident. But as he reached for the dial, a voice behind him stopped him cold.

"Yo, Kenneth," the voice called, smooth and deliberate. He turned to see a tall, broad-shouldered senior leaning casually against the lockers. His name was Darren, someone Kenneth had only interacted with in passing but knew by reputation. Darren was the kind of guy everyone noticed—confident, charismatic, and always the center of attention.

"What's up?" Kenneth asked cautiously, closing his locker.

Darren smirked, his eyes flicking down to Kenneth's sagging jeans and back up to his face. "Just wanted to talk. Seems like you've been catching a lot of heat lately."

Kenneth tensed. "Yeah, well, people love to talk."

"True," Darren said, stepping closer. "But sometimes it's about what you're giving them to talk about."

Kenneth frowned, his grip tightening on the strap of his backpack. "What's that supposed to mean?"

Darren leaned against the locker beside him, crossing his arms. "I'm just saying, you're out here sagging like you're on some Vicious V video set, but you're walking through a school full of people who don't get it. Makes you wonder what message you're trying to send."

Kenneth felt his stomach twist. "I'm not trying to send any message. This is just how I dress."

Darren raised an eyebrow. "Maybe. But you know how people are—they see the sagging, they think they know who you are. And if they're wrong... well, you're the one stuck dealing with it."

The words hung in the air, heavier than Kenneth wanted to admit. Darren wasn't laughing or mocking him like the others. His tone was calm, almost calculated, as if he was dissecting Kenneth's entire identity with surgical precision. It wasn't comforting—it was unnerving.

"So what?" Kenneth shot back. "I'm supposed to change how I dress just so people won't make stupid assumptions about me?"

Darren shrugged. "I didn't say that. I'm just saying, if you're gonna sag, you better own it. Otherwise, people are gonna think it's for them."

Kenneth's eyes narrowed. "What's that supposed to mean?"

Darren smirked again, this time with a hint of amusement. "Come on, Kenneth. You've heard the rumors. Guys saying you're sagging for attention, that maybe you're... you know."

Kenneth's face burned. "That's not true."

"I didn't say it was," Darren replied, holding his hands up. "But that's how people think. And unless you're ready to shut them down, those whispers aren't going anywhere."

Kenneth felt the frustration rising in his chest, his fists clenching at his sides. "Why do people even care so much? Why can't they just leave me alone?"

Darren's expression shifted, his smirk fading. "Because

standing out scares people. Makes them uncomfortable. And when people are uncomfortable, they lash out."

Kenneth stared at Darren, his anger giving way to confusion. "Why do you even care? You don't even know me."

Darren tilted his head, considering the question. "Maybe I've been there. Maybe I know what it's like to have people try to box you in just because you don't fit their mold."

Kenneth blinked, caught off guard. He had never thought of Darren as someone who dealt with anything remotely similar to what he was going through.

"Look," Darren said, his tone softening. "I'm not saying you should stop being yourself. But if you're gonna keep sagging, you gotta decide what it means to you. Because if you don't know, other people are gonna decide for you."

Kenneth nodded slowly, the words sinking in deeper than he wanted to admit. Darren gave him a pat on the shoulder before walking away, leaving Kenneth alone with his thoughts.

That evening, Kenneth sat on the edge of his bed, replaying the conversation in his mind. Darren's words lingered like an echo, forcing him to confront questions he had been avoiding. What did sagging mean to him? Was it just a way to feel connected to Vicious V, or was it something more?

He grabbed his journal from the nightstand, flipping to a blank page. The pen hovered over the paper for a moment before he began to write.

Dear Journal,

Today, someone asked me why I sag. Not directly, but that's what they meant. At first, I thought it was a stupid question. I sag because I want to. Because it's my style. But now I'm not so sure. Am I doing it because I like it, or because I want people to see me a certain way? And if they're seeing me the wrong way, is it still worth it?

I don't want to stop. Sagging feels like a part of who I am. But maybe I need to figure out who I am without it too.

He closed the journal, setting it back on the nightstand. The weight in his chest hadn't disappeared, but it felt different now—less like a burden and more like a challenge. Kenneth didn't have all the answers, but for the first time, he felt like he was asking the right questions.

Chapter 9: The Ambush

The hallway was unusually quiet as Kenneth walked toward his next class, his sneakers squeaking faintly against the linoleum floor. He was late, as usual, but today he welcomed the empty halls. No whispers, no stares, no tension crawling up his spine. Just silence. He adjusted his sagging jeans slightly, the familiar motion calming him, even as Darren's words from yesterday replayed in his mind.

What does it mean to you?

Kenneth hadn't come up with an answer yet. He just knew that pulling his pants up to avoid scrutiny didn't feel right. If he gave in now, wouldn't that mean they'd won?

He rounded the corner to his locker, ready to grab the notebook he'd forgotten earlier, when he heard it—the low murmur of voices just ahead. He tensed instinctively, slowing his pace. As he approached, he realized the voices weren't friendly. They were waiting for him.

"Well, look who finally showed up," a familiar voice drawled. Kenneth's heart sank. It was Marcus, one of the athletes who'd been at the center of the teasing about his pants. Marcus leaned against the lockers, arms crossed, his smirk radiating cocky energy.

Behind him, two other guys—Todd and Jamal—stood like shadows, flanking him on either side. Kenneth stopped, gripping the strap of his backpack tighter. "What do you want?" he asked, his voice steady, though his heart raced.

Marcus pushed off the locker and took a step closer. "Just wanted to talk," he said, his tone dripping with mock sincerity. "We've been noticing you, Kenny. You've got... style."

Kenneth felt the heat rising in his face, but he forced himself to stay calm. "Yeah? What's your point?"

Marcus grinned, the kind of grin that made Kenneth's stomach churn. "Just wondering who you're sagging for. 'Cause it sure looks like you're putting on a show."

The words hit harder than Kenneth expected, his breath catching in his throat. He knew what Marcus was implying—what they'd all been whispering behind his back. "I'm not sagging for anyone," Kenneth said, his voice low but firm. "This is just me."

Todd snickered from the side. "Yeah, right. You've been strutting around like you're waiting for someone to notice. Don't act like you don't know."

Kenneth took a step back, his fingers tightening around the strap of his backpack. He wanted to walk away, but his feet felt rooted to the spot. "You don't know anything about me."

Marcus tilted his head, his smirk widening. "Oh, I think we

know plenty. You wanna act tough, but you're out here sagging like you're... advertising something. Maybe you should be a little more honest with yourself."

The words hung in the air, heavier than Kenneth could bear. He could feel his anger bubbling, his fists itching to lash out, but he forced himself to take a deep breath. "You don't get to define me," he said, his voice sharp. "Not you, not anyone."

Marcus raised an eyebrow, as if Kenneth's defiance was amusing. "Alright, Kenny. Whatever you say." He stepped back, gesturing for Todd and Jamal to follow him. "But you should think about what you're putting out there. People are watching."

The three of them walked away, their laughter echoing down the hallway. Kenneth stood frozen, his mind racing. Every part of him wanted to scream, to chase after them and demand they take it back, but he didn't. Instead, he turned to his locker, yanked it open, and grabbed his notebook. His hands trembled as he slammed the door shut and walked to class.

By the time the lunch bell rang, Kenneth still hadn't shaken the encounter. He sat alone at a table in the corner of the cafeteria, picking at his food. Malik and E-Money had waved him over earlier, but he'd brushed them off, mumbling something about needing space.

The cafeteria was a blur of noise and movement, but Kenneth barely noticed. His mind replayed Marcus's words over and over, each repetition stoking the fire in his chest.

"Hey, Kenny," a voice said, breaking through his thoughts. He looked up to see Darren standing across from him, a tray in his hands. "Mind if I sit?"

Kenneth hesitated, then shrugged. "Sure."

Darren slid into the seat across from him, studying Kenneth for a moment before speaking. “You look like you’ve had a rough day.”

Kenneth scoffed. “That obvious, huh?”

Darren nodded. “You wanna talk about it?”

Kenneth considered brushing him off, but something about Darren’s steady gaze made him pause. He sighed, leaning back in his chair. “It’s the same crap. People saying stuff about my pants, making assumptions about me. It’s like they’re obsessed.”

Darren nodded slowly. “Yeah, people love to project their insecurities onto someone else. Makes them feel bigger.”

Kenneth frowned. “What’s their problem, though? I’m not hurting anyone. Why do they care so much?”

“Because you’re different,” Darren said simply. “And different scares people. They can’t handle it, so they try to break you down.”

Kenneth looked at him, frustration flickering in his eyes. “So what am I supposed to do? Just let them keep coming at me?”

Darren shook his head. “No. You stand your ground. But you also decide what’s worth your energy. Sometimes proving people wrong isn’t about what you say or do—it’s about being unapologetically yourself.”

Kenneth absorbed the words, unsure if he agreed but grateful for the perspective. “Easier said than done,” he muttered.

Darren smirked. “Most things are.”

That evening, Kenneth walked home with his hands stuffed in his hoodie pockets, his sagging jeans swaying with each step. The confrontation with Marcus still gnawed at him, but Darren's words gave him something to hold onto. He wasn't sure what standing his ground looked like, but he knew he couldn't keep letting their words dictate his feelings.

When he got home, Carla was in the kitchen, stirring a pot on the stove. She looked up as he walked in, her expression softening. "Hey, baby. You okay?"

Kenneth nodded, dropping his bag on the couch. "Yeah. Just tired."

Carla wiped her hands on a towel and walked over, placing a hand on his shoulder. "You know you can talk to me, right? About anything."

Kenneth hesitated, then nodded again. "I know."

Carla studied him for a moment, then smiled. "Alright. Dinner'll be ready in twenty."

Kenneth headed to his room, collapsing onto his bed. He stared at the ceiling for a long moment before grabbing his journal from the nightstand. He flipped to a blank page, his pen moving almost before he'd decided what to write.

Dear Journal,

Today was rough. Marcus and his crew decided to come at me again, saying stuff about my pants, about what they think it means. It's like they're determined to make me feel small, like I don't belong. But I'm tired of feeling like I have to prove myself to them.

Darren said something today that stuck with me. He said proving people wrong isn't always about what you say—it's about being yourself, even when it's hard. I don't know if I'm there yet, but I want to be. I want to feel like me without needing anyone else's approval.

I sag because it makes me feel like me. And maybe that's enough.

Kenneth set the journal aside and exhaled slowly. The fire in his chest hadn't gone out, but it felt manageable now—a spark instead of an inferno. He didn't have all the answers, but he was starting to believe he didn't need them. Not yet, anyway.

Chapter 10: The Aftermath

Kenneth sat on the edge of his bed, his shoulders hunched, staring at the blank wall in front of him. The events of the day played on repeat in his head, each moment sharper and more painful than the last. Marcus's smirk. The mocking laughter of his friends. Their words—cutting, loaded, and dripping with implications Kenneth wasn't ready to confront.

He leaned forward, resting his elbows on his knees and burying his face in his hands. For years, sagging had been more than just a style choice for him—it had been his armor. A way to express himself in a world that often felt like it wasn't made for him. But now, that armor felt like it was cracking. Each comment, each stare, each whisper chipped away at it, leaving him vulnerable and raw.

"Why does it even matter?" he muttered to himself, his voice barely above a whisper. The question hung in the air, unanswered. Why did something as simple as how he wore his pants cause so much noise? It wasn't like he was hurting anyone. It was his body, his choice. Why did everyone else feel entitled to an opinion?

A soft knock at his door pulled him out of his thoughts. Carla stepped in, her brow furrowed with concern. She didn't say anything at first, just crossed the room and sat beside him on the bed. Her presence was grounding, and when she placed a warm hand on his back, the dam Kenneth had been holding back all day finally broke.

"I'm so tired of this, Ma," he said, his voice cracking as tears welled up in his eyes. "Tired of people acting like they know me. Like they can just... define me because of how I look."

Carla's hand moved in slow, soothing circles. "I know, baby," she said gently. "I know it's not fair."

"It's not just unfair," Kenneth said, sitting up and turning to face her. "It's like... no matter what I do, they're always gonna see me how they want to. I'm just some kid with sagging pants to them. Either I'm a thug, or I'm... I'm something I'm not."

Carla's expression softened. She reached up to cup his face with her hands, her thumbs brushing away a tear that had escaped down his cheek. "Listen to me, Kenneth. You are more than what people see on the surface. More than their assumptions. But I also know that doesn't make it hurt any less."

Kenneth swallowed hard, his chest tightening. "I just want them to stop," he whispered. "I just want to be left alone."

Carla nodded, her hands falling to her lap. "I get that, baby. I really do. But sometimes, the world doesn't give us that choice. Sometimes, we have to decide who we are in spite of what they say."

Kenneth looked away, her words heavy in his mind. He

wanted to believe her. He wanted to feel strong enough to fight through it, but he didn't. Not yet.

The next morning, Kenneth woke up feeling drained. He went through the motions of his routine—showering, getting dressed, forcing himself to eat a bowl of cereal—but everything felt mechanical. As he walked to school, the weight of the previous day settled over him like a heavy coat. He pulled his hoodie over his head, hoping to shrink into himself, to disappear.

But the moment he stepped into the hallway, the tension was back. He felt the stares, the whispers, the way people seemed to watch his every move. He forced himself to walk with his head up, but inside, he was crumbling.

"Hey, Kenny!" a voice called from behind him. He turned to see Malik jogging to catch up, his expression concerned.

"What's up?" Kenneth asked, trying to sound casual, though his voice came out flat.

"I was gonna ask you the same thing," Malik said, falling into step beside him. "You've been off since yesterday. Everything cool?"

Kenneth hesitated. He wanted to brush it off, to pretend everything was fine, but the words were stuck in his throat. Finally, he sighed. "Not really."

"Wanna talk about it?" Malik asked, his tone gentle.

Kenneth looked around the crowded hallway before answering. "It's just... Marcus and his crew. They said some stuff yesterday that got to me."

"What kind of stuff?" Malik's tone shifted, his concern giving way to quiet anger.

Kenneth hesitated again, unsure if he wanted to say it out loud. “They... they said I’m sagging for attention. That maybe I’m... you know.”

Malik stopped walking, forcing Kenneth to do the same. He looked at him, his jaw tight. “Man, screw those guys. They don’t know what they’re talking about.”

Kenneth laughed bitterly. “Yeah, but that doesn’t stop them from saying it.”

“They say it ‘cause they’re scared,” Malik said, his voice firm. “They don’t get it, so they try to tear you down. But that’s not about you—it’s about them.”

Kenneth wanted to believe him, but the doubt lingered. “What if they’re right?” he asked quietly. “What if I’m just making things harder for myself?”

Malik shook his head. “Nah, man. You’re being yourself. That’s never wrong. And if they can’t handle that, that’s their problem, not yours.”

Kenneth nodded slowly, Malik’s words sinking in. He didn’t have all the answers, but maybe he didn’t need them right now. Maybe it was enough to just keep going.

By lunchtime, Kenneth was sitting with Malik, E-Money, and a few others. The cafeteria was loud, filled with the usual buzz of conversation and laughter, but for the first time all day, Kenneth felt a little lighter. The guys were cracking jokes, teasing each other, and for a while, Kenneth was able to forget the tension hanging over him.

“Man, you’re a disaster in the kitchen,” Malik said, shaking his head at E-Money.

"Hey, at least I tried," E-Money shot back, grinning. "Can't say the same for some people."

Kenneth chuckled, the sound surprising even him. It felt good to laugh, to let go of the weight on his chest, even if only for a little while.

That evening, Kenneth sat at his desk, his journal open in front of him. The blank page stared back at him, daring him to put his thoughts into words. He picked up his pen, hesitated for a moment, and then began to write.

Dear Journal,

Today was better. Not great, but better. I'm still mad at Marcus and his crew for what they said. I don't think I'll ever forget it. But I'm starting to realize that maybe their opinions don't matter as much as I thought they did.

Malik said something today that stuck with me. He said being yourself is never wrong. I want to believe that. I want to believe that I can just be me, sagging pants and all, and that's enough.

It's not easy, though. Some days, it feels like the whole world is against me. But maybe I don't have to fight the whole world. Maybe I just have to fight for me.

Kenneth closed the journal, setting it aside with a sigh. The fire in his chest wasn't gone, but it had dimmed to a manageable glow. For now, that was enough.

Chapter 11: The Realization

Kenneth sat at his desk, staring out the window as a warm breeze rattled the blinds. Outside, kids laughed and played basketball on the school's cracked court, their voices rising and falling in a rhythmic hum. It was lunchtime, but Kenneth had chosen to stay in class, away from the whispers, the stares, and the constant commentary that seemed to follow him everywhere.

Sagging pants. Who would've thought something so simple could make him a target? It was just fabric, a choice he made because it felt like him. But to everyone else, it was a symbol—one they thought they had the right to define.

Kenneth slouched lower in his seat, glancing down at the way his jeans hung loosely on his hips. He liked the way they fit, the way they moved when he walked. They reminded him of the rappers he admired, the ones who carried themselves with a confidence he wanted to embody. But lately, the pants felt heavier, like they carried more than just his style—they carried everyone else's assumptions.

The door creaked open, and Malik stepped in, his lunch tray balanced in one hand. "Kenny, man, what are you doing in here?" he asked, setting the tray down on the desk next to Kenneth.

Kenneth shrugged, avoiding Malik's gaze. "Just needed some space."

Malik leaned back in his chair, unwrapping his sandwich. "Space, huh? Or are you hiding?"

Kenneth shot him a glare. "I'm not hiding."

Malik held up his hands in surrender. "Alright, alright. Just asking. But you know, sitting in here by yourself isn't gonna make it stop."

Kenneth sighed, his fingers drumming on the desk. "You think I don't know that? It's not about making it stop. I just... I don't know, man. I'm tired of it. Tired of people acting like they know me because of my pants."

Malik nodded, chewing thoughtfully. "Yeah, I get that. People love to talk. They see something different, and they don't know what to do with it, so they make it a big deal."

Kenneth leaned forward, resting his elbows on the desk. "But why, though? It's not like I'm the only one who sags. Half the guys out there do it. So why does it feel like I'm the only one catching all this heat?"

Malik shrugged. "Maybe it's because you do it with style."

Kenneth snorted, shaking his head. "Style, huh? Doesn't feel like it."

Malik grinned, leaning in closer. "Think about it, though. You walk down the hall like you own it. You don't try to hide who you are. That scares people, man. Makes them uncomfortable. So they try to bring you down."

Kenneth let the words sink in, his gaze drifting back to the window. Did he walk like he owned it? He wasn't sure anymore. Lately, he felt more like he was walking on eggshells, trying to avoid the next comment, the next stare.

After school, Kenneth walked home with his hands stuffed deep into his hoodie pockets. His jeans hung low, swaying with each step, and he couldn't help but feel like every passing car, every pedestrian, was watching him. Judging him. It wasn't paranoia—it was experience.

As he turned the corner onto his street, a voice called out from behind him. “Hey, Kenny! Wait up!”

He turned to see E-Money jogging toward him, his backpack bouncing against his shoulders. Kenneth slowed his pace, waiting for him to catch up.

“What’s good?” E-Money asked, falling into step beside him.

Kenneth shrugged. “Same old.”

E-Money tilted his head, giving Kenneth a sidelong glance. “Still tripping over what Marcus and them said?”

Kenneth stiffened, the memory flashing through his mind. “It’s not just them,” he muttered. “It’s everyone. Everywhere I go, it’s like people can’t stop staring at me. Whispering.”

E-Money nodded, his expression thoughtful. “Yeah, people are wild like that. But you can’t let it get to you, man. You gotta own it.”

Kenneth frowned. “Own what?”

“The sag,” E-Money said, gesturing to Kenneth’s jeans. “You rock it like nobody else, but if you don’t believe in it, people are gonna see that. They’re gonna smell that doubt, and they’ll use it against you.”

Kenneth shook his head, frustration bubbling to the surface. “But why do I have to prove anything? Why can’t people just let me be?”

E-Money paused, his hands slipping into his pockets. “Because people are scared of what they don’t understand. You sag your pants because it’s you, right? It’s how you express yourself. But they don’t see that. They just see a stereotype."

Kenneth kicked at a loose pebble on the sidewalk, his jaw tightening. "Yeah, well, I'm tired of being a stereotype."

E-Money clapped a hand on Kenneth's shoulder. "Then show them you're more than that. You don't have to change who you are, but you do have to decide what it means to you. Because if you don't, they're gonna decide for you."

Later that evening, Kenneth sat at his desk, staring at his open journal. The blank page seemed to mock him, daring him to put his thoughts into words. He picked up his pen, hesitated, then began to write.

Dear Journal,

I don't know why this is so hard. It's just pants. That's what I keep telling myself. It's just pants. But it's not, is it? Not to everyone else. To them, it's a statement. A message. But I never meant it to be that. I just like how they feel, how they look. I like the way they move when I walk.

But now it feels like everyone wants to tell me what they mean. Marcus and his crew think it makes me weak, makes me a target. The teachers think it makes me trouble. Some of the guys at school think it makes me... something else.

I don't know what to do anymore. E-Money says I have to own it, but how do I own something when I don't even know what it means to me?

Kenneth put the pen down, leaning back in his chair. The words on the page stared back at him, raw and unpolished, but true. He didn't have the answers yet, but at least he was starting to ask the right questions.

The next day, Kenneth decided to take E-Money's advice. He walked into school with his head held high, his jeans hanging low as always. The stares were still there, the whispers still followed him, but he didn't let them weigh him down. Instead, he focused on the rhythm of his steps, the sway of his pants, the steady beat of his heart.

When he reached his locker, he found Marcus leaning against it, his arms crossed and a smirk on his face. Kenneth felt his chest tighten, but he didn't stop. He walked straight up to his locker, meeting Marcus's gaze head-on.

"Morning, Kenny," Marcus said, his voice dripping with mock sweetness. "Still showing off for us, huh?"

Kenneth didn't flinch. He didn't look away. Instead, he shrugged, a small smile tugging at the corner of his mouth. "Nah, man. I'm just being me. But thanks for noticing."

Marcus blinked, caught off guard by Kenneth's response. For a moment, he seemed at a loss for words. Then he pushed off the locker, shaking his head with a chuckle. "Alright, Kenny. Have it your way."

As Marcus walked away, Kenneth felt a small spark of pride in his chest. It wasn't a victory—not yet—but it was a step. And for now, that was enough.

Chapter 12: The Lesson

Kenneth stared out of the classroom window, his mind miles away from the droning voice of his history teacher. The textbook on his desk lay unopened, its pages untouched. Around him, students whispered, giggled, and scrolled through their phones, but Kenneth barely noticed. He felt trapped—caged by the stares, the whispers, and the weight of everything that had happened over the past weeks.

Sagging pants. It had started as a way to express himself, a tribute to the rappers he admired, a small rebellion against conformity. But now, it felt like a curse. No matter what he did, he couldn't escape the judgment, the assumptions, the consequences. He had tried to hold his head high, to own his style, but the effort was exhausting.

The final bell rang, jolting Kenneth from his thoughts. As the students poured out of the room, Kenneth stayed seated, staring at his reflection in the smudged window.

"Mr. Gilbert," the teacher's voice broke in, sharp and irritated. "Unless you plan on repeating this grade, I suggest you pay more attention in class."

Kenneth didn't reply. He grabbed his backpack and slung it over one shoulder, his jeans sagging low as he shuffled toward the door. The teacher sighed loudly, muttering something about "lost causes," but Kenneth didn't look back.

The hallway was alive with noise—lockers slamming, shoes squeaking on linoleum, and the chatter of students. Kenneth kept his head down as he walked, avoiding eye contact. But even with his hood up and his pace quick, he couldn't escape the comments.

"Yo, Kenny! Still sagging for the crowd, huh?" someone called.

"Better pull those pants up before you trip," another voice jeered.

Kenneth's jaw tightened, but he kept walking. He had heard it all before. He turned a corner and headed toward the exit, desperate to escape the suffocating walls of the school.

Outside, the afternoon sun was warm on his skin, but it didn't ease the tension in his chest. Kenneth leaned against the brick wall, staring at the cracked pavement beneath his sneakers. He felt like he was standing at a crossroads, though he couldn't quite see the paths ahead.

That evening, Kenneth sat at the kitchen table, pushing food around his plate while his mother, Carla, scrubbed dishes at the sink. The clatter of plates and the hum of running water filled the silence, but Carla's watchful eyes kept flicking toward him.

"What's going on, Kenneth?" she asked finally, turning off the water and drying her hands. "You've been quiet lately."

Kenneth shrugged, not meeting her gaze. "Just tired."

Carla pulled out a chair and sat across from him, her expression soft but firm. "It's more than that. Talk to me."

Kenneth hesitated, his fork frozen mid-air. He wanted to tell her everything—to unload the frustration, the anger, the exhaustion. But he knew what she would say, and he didn't want to hear it.

"It's nothing," he mumbled. "School's just... school."

Carla studied him for a moment, her brow furrowing. "Kenneth, I know you've been having a hard time. But you can't just shut down. You're smart, and you've got so much potential. Don't let—"

"Don't let what?" Kenneth cut in, his voice sharp. "Don't let them win? Don't let the haters get to me? You think I haven't heard all that before? It doesn't change anything, Ma."

Carla's mouth tightened, but she didn't look away. "Dropping out isn't the answer, Kenneth."

"I didn't say I was dropping out," Kenneth shot back, though the thought had been circling his mind for weeks. "But maybe school isn't for me."

"Don't say that," Carla said, her voice trembling slightly. "School is your way out, Kenneth. Your way to something better."

Kenneth stood abruptly, his chair scraping loudly against the floor. "Better? Better than what? Better than this?" He gestured around the modest kitchen, his frustration spilling over. "What's the point if nothing ever changes?"

Carla stood too, her eyes flashing. "The point is that you don't give up on yourself! Because if you do, no one else is going to fight for you."

The words hung in the air, heavy and sharp. Kenneth stared at her, his chest heaving, before turning and walking toward the door.

"I need some air," he muttered, grabbing his hoodie and stepping outside before she could respond.

The streets were quiet as Kenneth walked aimlessly, his mind racing. Carla's words rang in his ears, but they felt distant, muffled by the weight of his own doubts. He had tried—tried to make it work, tried to push through. But no matter how hard he tried, it always felt like he was running in circles, getting nowhere.

As he rounded a corner, a familiar voice called out from a nearby porch. "Yo, Kenny! What's good, man?"

Kenneth looked up to see J-Roc, a neighborhood hustler known for always having cash and connections. J-Roc was leaning against a railing, a blunt in one hand and a gold chain glinting around his neck.

Kenneth hesitated, then walked over. “Not much,” he said, shoving his hands into his hoodie pockets.

J-Roc took a drag and exhaled slowly, the smoke curling into the night air. “You look like you got a lot on your mind. What’s up?”

Kenneth shrugged. “Just tired of all the bull at school.”

J-Roc nodded knowingly. “Yeah, I hear that. School ain’t for everybody, you feel me? Some of us gotta find other ways to make it.”

Kenneth glanced at him, his curiosity piqued. “Like what?”

J-Roc smirked, tapping ash off the end of his blunt. “Like this.” He gestured to himself—the chain, the watch, the sneakers. “Ain’t nobody at school teaching you how to get this kind of money.”

Kenneth frowned, the words sinking in. He had always been wary of J-Roc’s lifestyle, but in that moment, it felt like a door was opening—one that led away from the frustration and judgment of school.

“What about the risks?” Kenneth asked cautiously.

J-Roc chuckled, shaking his head. “Life’s a risk, Kenny. Question is, you gonna play it safe and stay broke, or you gonna take control?”

Kenneth didn’t respond, but his silence spoke volumes.

When Kenneth got home that night, Carla was waiting for him

in the living room, her arms crossed and her expression tight with worry. But he didn't stop to talk. He went straight to his room, closing the door behind him. As he sat on the edge of his bed, J-Roc's words echoed in his mind.

"Take control."

For the first time in weeks, it felt like there was a way out. It wasn't the way Carla wanted for him, but it was a way.

Kenneth leaned back against the wall, staring at the ceiling. He knew the decision he was making wasn't without consequences. But at that moment, it felt like the only choice he had.

Chapter 13: The Transformation

Kenneth leaned against a chain-link fence at the corner of his block, his hoodie pulled low over his face. His sagging jeans swayed slightly in the evening breeze, and the sound of distant sirens hummed in the background. J-Roc stood a few feet away, casually lighting another blunt, his gold chain glinting under the streetlight.

"You ready, Kenny?" J-Roc asked, exhaling a slow stream of smoke. His tone was casual, but there was an edge to it, as if he were testing Kenneth's resolve.

Kenneth hesitated, the weight of the decision pressing down on him. He had been here before—standing at the edge of something he couldn't fully see, torn between what he knew was right and what felt like the only way forward. Carla's voice echoed in his mind, sharp and pleading, but he pushed it aside.

"I'm ready," he said finally, his voice steady.

J-Roc grinned, handing Kenneth a small plastic bag filled with powder. "Good. Start small. Keep it simple. Don't get greedy."

Kenneth nodded, pocketing the bag. His heart pounded as he walked away, his mind racing with a mix of excitement and dread. This was it. The start of something new—something dangerous, but something that felt like control.

The first few weeks passed in a blur. Kenneth quickly learned the ropes, sticking to the rules J-Roc had drilled into him: stay low-key, don't flash cash, and never trust anyone too easily. The money came fast—faster than he had expected—and with it came a new sense of power. For the first time, Kenneth felt like he was in control of his life, like he didn't have to answer to anyone.

But the thrill didn't come without its costs. The weight of the plastic bags in his pockets felt heavier with each passing day, and the looks he got from people in the neighborhood—some wary, some admiring—only added to the pressure. Every glance felt like a question, every conversation a potential threat.

One night, as Kenneth counted a stack of cash in his room, Carla knocked on the door. He quickly shoved the money into his backpack and opened the door just enough to see her face.

"Dinner's ready," she said, her tone softer than usual. "I made your favorite—fried chicken."

Kenneth nodded, avoiding her gaze. "I'll be out in a minute."

Carla lingered for a moment, her eyes searching his face. "You've been out a lot lately," she said. "Hanging with J-Roc and those boys."

Kenneth tensed. “So?”

Carla sighed, leaning against the doorframe. “So, I know what they’re about, Kenneth. And I know you’re smarter than that.”

Kenneth felt a flash of anger rise in his chest. “You don’t know anything about them.”

“I know enough,” Carla shot back. “And I know you. You’re not like them, Kenneth. You don’t have to be.”

Kenneth clenched his fists, struggling to keep his voice steady. “Maybe I don’t want to be who you think I am.”

Carla’s expression softened, but her eyes were filled with worry. “I just want you to be safe. That’s all.”

Kenneth didn’t reply. He closed the door gently, locking it behind him. As he sat back on his bed, the money still hidden in his backpack, he felt a pang of guilt. But he pushed it away, telling himself that this was his life now—his choice.

By the time winter rolled around, Kenneth had become a fixture in J-Roc’s crew. He had regular customers, a steady income, and a growing reputation. But the tension in his chest never fully went away. He found himself looking over his shoulder more often, his sagging jeans now a symbol of both his defiance and his vulnerability.

One evening, Kenneth was standing on the corner when a black sedan pulled up. The window rolled down, revealing a man in his late twenties with a cold, calculating gaze.

“You Kenny?” the man asked.

Kenneth nodded, his pulse quickening. “Yeah. Who’s asking?”

The man smirked. “I’m Rico. J-Roc said you’re reliable. I got a job for you.”

Kenneth hesitated, glancing toward J-Roc, who was leaning against a nearby wall, watching the exchange. J-Roc gave him a slight nod, signaling his approval.

“What kind of job?” Kenneth asked.

Rico’s smirk widened. “Nothing too heavy. Just a delivery. Easy money.”

Kenneth swallowed hard, nodding again. “Alright. I’m in.”

The delivery went smoothly, but the encounter left Kenneth feeling uneasy. Rico’s presence had been intimidating, and Kenneth couldn’t shake the feeling that he was being pulled deeper into a world he didn’t fully understand. But the money was good—too good to walk away from.

Over the next few months, Kenneth’s life became a cycle of late nights, quick exchanges, and constant vigilance. The cash piled up, but so did the stress. He started skipping meals, sleeping less, and growing more paranoid. Even his sagging jeans, once a source of pride, now felt like a liability—something that made him stand out in a way he couldn’t afford.

One night, as Kenneth walked home from a deal, he spotted a patrol car parked at the end of the block. His heart raced as he slipped into an alley, his hand instinctively going to the waistband of his jeans, making sure the bag he was carrying was secure.

“Yo, Kenny!” a voice called, startling him. He turned to see J-Roc jogging toward him, his face tense.

"What's up?" Kenneth asked, trying to keep his voice calm.

"Cops are circling," J-Roc said, glancing over his shoulder. "Lay low for a while."

Kenneth nodded, his pulse pounding in his ears. As he walked the rest of the way home, his mind raced with thoughts of what could happen if he got caught. Carla's face flashed in his mind, and for a moment, he felt a pang of regret. But he shook it off, telling himself that this was the life he had chosen—and he had to see it through.

Chapter 14: The Arrest

The weight of Kenneth's decisions seemed to press down on him as he stood on the corner of the block, the cold evening air biting at his face. His hands were buried deep in the pockets of his hoodie, fingers nervously brushing against the plastic bag tucked into his waistband. Across the street, J-Roc leaned against a lamppost, his gold chain gleaming in the dim light as he chatted with Rico. Kenneth kept his eyes on them, waiting for the signal to move.

"Yo, Kenny!" J-Roc called, waving him over. Kenneth glanced around, ensuring no one was watching too closely, before crossing the street.

"You good?" J-Roc asked, lowering his voice as Kenneth approached.

"Yeah, I'm good," Kenneth replied, though his stomach churned with unease.

Rico handed Kenneth a brown paper bag, its weight heavier than he expected. "Same spot as usual," Rico said, his tone curt. "Make it quick."

Kenneth nodded, slipping the bag into his backpack. As he turned to leave, J-Roc grabbed his shoulder, pulling him close.

"Keep your head up, Kenny," J-Roc said, his voice low. "You're in this now. Don't let nobody shake you."

Kenneth nodded again, though his heart pounded in his chest. He adjusted his sagging jeans and started walking, his steps quick and purposeful. The streetlights flickered overhead, casting long shadows that seemed to follow him.

The spot was a small alleyway a few blocks away, tucked between two run-down buildings. Kenneth had been here countless times before, the graffiti-covered walls and overflowing trash bins now a familiar backdrop to his new life. He leaned against the wall, pulling out his phone to send the signal to his contact.

As he waited, the minutes dragged on, each second stretching into an eternity. The sound of distant sirens made his pulse quicken, though he told himself they had nothing to do with him.

Finally, a figure emerged from the shadows, a man in his mid-30s with a scruffy beard and a leather jacket. Kenneth recognized him as a regular—someone who always paid on time and never caused trouble.

"You got it?" the man asked, his voice gruff.

Kenneth nodded, reaching into his backpack and pulling out the paper bag. He handed it over quickly, avoiding the man's gaze.

"Good looking out," the man said, slipping a wad of cash into Kenneth's hand. Kenneth stuffed the money into his pocket and turned to leave, his steps quickening as he put distance between himself and the transaction.

Kenneth was only a block from home when he saw the flashing lights. His heart stopped as two squad cars turned the corner, their headlights cutting through the darkness. He froze, unsure whether to run or stay put, but the decision was made for him when the cars skidded to a stop, and officers poured out, guns drawn.

"Hands in the air!" one of them shouted, his voice sharp and commanding.

Kenneth's breath came in short, panicked gasps as he raised his hands, the plastic bag in his waistband suddenly feeling like a lead weight. The officers moved quickly, surrounding him and pinning him against the wall. His hoodie was yanked back, and his backpack was ripped from his shoulders.

"What's this?" an officer sneered, pulling the brown paper bag from the backpack. He opened it, revealing several smaller bags of powder.

Kenneth didn't respond. His mind raced as he struggled to process what was happening.

"Looks like we got ourselves a dealer," another officer said, his voice laced with satisfaction.

Kenneth clenched his jaw, fighting back the urge to say something—anything—that might make this worse. But the words wouldn't come. He felt the cold steel of handcuffs snap around his wrists, the weight of them a harsh reminder of the reality he now faced.

The ride to the station was a blur. Kenneth sat in the back of the squad car, his sagging jeans bunched awkwardly around his knees as he stared out the window. The city lights flickered past, each one feeling like a distant memory of a life he'd left behind.

At the station, he was fingerprinted, photographed, and processed with a mechanical efficiency that made him feel more like an object than a person. The other detainees eyed him warily as he was led to a holding cell, the clanging of the metal door echoing in his ears.

Kenneth sat on the cold bench, his head in his hands. The weight of everything—his choices, his mistakes, his future—pressed down on him like a crushing tide. He thought of Carla, of the way she had begged him to stay on the right path, and felt a pang of guilt so sharp it nearly took his breath away.

Hours later, Kenneth found himself sitting across from a public defender, a tired-looking woman with a stack of files and a no-nonsense demeanor.

"First offense?" she asked, flipping through his paperwork.

Kenneth nodded, his voice barely above a whisper. "Yeah."

The woman sighed, leaning back in her chair. "You're looking at a minimum of five years, depending on how cooperative you are."

Kenneth's stomach churned. "Five years?" he echoed, his voice trembling.

The woman nodded. "You're lucky it's not more. Federal drug charges are serious, Kenneth. The judge isn't going to go easy on you."

Kenneth sat back, his mind racing. Five years. The words echoed in his head, each one a hammer blow to the fragile hope he had clung to. How had it come to this? How had he let it get this far?

The courtroom was a blur of faces and voices, the judge's gavel cutting through the noise like a blade. Kenneth stood beside his attorney, his hands trembling as the charges were read aloud. Carla sat in the back of the room, her face pale and drawn, tears streaming silently down her cheeks.

When the sentence was handed down—five years in federal prison—Kenneth felt a strange sense of detachment, as if the words were happening to someone else. He barely registered the guards leading him away, the cold metal of the cuffs once again biting into his wrists.

As the prison gates loomed ahead, Kenneth couldn't help but think of the choices that had brought him here. The sagging pants that had once been a symbol of his defiance now felt like a cruel reminder of the life he had tried to claim—and the one he had lost.

Chapter 15: The Prison Warning

Kenneth stepped off the transport bus, the thick steel door slamming shut behind him. He squinted against the harsh sunlight as the armed guards barked orders, their voices echoing off the concrete walls of the federal penitentiary. Around him, a group of inmates shuffled forward in their shackles, heads down, their expressions a mixture of resignation and defiance.

The air smelled of sweat, metal, and something faintly medicinal, and Kenneth's chest tightened as he took in the looming watchtowers and razor wire stretching across the sky. This was his new reality.

The guards led them inside, where the sterile fluorescents

cast a harsh glow over the intake area. One by one, the inmates were processed, stripped of their belongings, and issued prison uniforms—standard orange jumpsuits. Kenneth's sagging jeans and hoodie were taken away, folded, and stored in a bag with his inmate ID scrawled across the label.

As he pulled on the stiff prison-issued clothes, a sense of vulnerability washed over him. Gone were the familiar comforts of his old life, replaced by the cold, unyielding walls of a system that now controlled every part of his existence.

By the time Kenneth was led to his cell, he was exhausted. His new bunkmate, a wiry man in his 40s with tattoos snaking up his arms, barely glanced up as Kenneth entered.

"Fresh meat," the man muttered, his voice tinged with both amusement and warning. "Better keep your head down."

Kenneth ignored him, tossing the thin mattress onto his bunk and lying down. He closed his eyes, hoping to block out the noise of the prison—a constant hum of voices, footsteps, and clanging metal.

But sleep didn't come easily. His mind was a storm of regret, fear, and defiance. He thought about his mother, her tear-streaked face as the judge handed down his sentence. He thought about J-Roc and Rico, both of whom had escaped unscathed. And he thought about himself—how he had let his choices lead him here.

The next day, during recreation time in the yard, Kenneth found himself sitting alone on a bench near the chain-link fence. He watched as groups of inmates clustered together—some lifting weights, others pacing the perimeter, and a few playing cards under the shade of a tree. The air was thick with tension, every movement laced with unspoken rules and hierarchy.

“Yo, newbie,” a voice called.

Kenneth turned to see a tall, broad-shouldered man walking toward him. His face was weathered, his eyes sharp and calculating. Kenneth tensed as the man stopped in front of him, crossing his arms.

“Name’s Big Ray,” the man said. “You’re new, so I’m gonna do you a favor. Call it... advice.”

Kenneth raised an eyebrow but said nothing, waiting for the man to continue.

Big Ray leaned in slightly, lowering his voice. “You sag your pants in here, boy?”

Kenneth frowned, confused. “What? No. Not since they took my stuff.”

Big Ray smirked, but there was no humor in his eyes. “Good. ‘Cause in here, sagging ain’t about fashion. It’s about sending a message—a message you don’t wanna send.”

Kenneth tilted his head, still not fully understanding. “What message?”

Big Ray’s expression hardened, and he glanced around to make sure no one was listening. “In here, sagging your pants means you’re available. You’re telling the other inmates you’re open for business. And by business, I mean you’re offering yourself up for sex.”

Kenneth’s stomach dropped. “You serious?”

“Dead serious,” Big Ray said, his tone leaving no room for

doubt. “Some of these guys, they’re predators. They see sagging, they think you’re easy prey. You don’t wanna give them that idea.”

Kenneth felt a wave of nausea roll over him as the implications sank in. He thought about how sagging had been such a big part of his identity on the outside—a way to express himself, to show confidence and defiance. Here, it was something entirely different. Something dangerous.

“So what do I do?” Kenneth asked, his voice low.

Big Ray straightened, his eyes narrowing. “You keep your pants up. You walk tall, you stay quiet, and you don’t give anyone a reason to look at you sideways. Prison’s all about survival, kid. You don’t survive by making yourself a target.”

Kenneth nodded slowly, the gravity of Big Ray’s words sinking in. “Thanks,” he said, though the word felt inadequate.

Big Ray grunted, turning to leave. “Don’t thank me. Just remember what I said.”

That night, Kenneth lay awake in his bunk, staring at the ceiling. Big Ray’s warning played over and over in his mind, each word carving deeper into his consciousness. He thought about the freedom he’d once taken for granted, the way he used to walk the halls of his school with his jeans sagging low, daring anyone to challenge him. Here, that same act could cost him more than his pride—it could cost him his safety, his dignity, even his life.

He glanced down at the waistband of his jumpsuit, the elastic snug against his hips. For the first time, he was grateful for its plainness, its uniformity. It offered him a kind of protection he hadn’t realized he needed.

The next day, Kenneth kept his head down as he moved through the routine—meals, recreation, work duty. He noticed the way some of the other inmates walked, their pants hanging low, the fabric pooling around their ankles. Some of them did it defiantly, daring anyone to say something. Others seemed oblivious, unaware of the message they were sending.

Big Ray's voice echoed in his mind: You don't survive by making yourself a target.

Kenneth tightened his grip on his tray as he passed through the cafeteria, his eyes scanning the room for potential threats. He was beginning to understand the unspoken rules of this place—the delicate balance of power and perception that dictated every interaction.

One evening, as Kenneth sat on his bunk, his bunkmate—a wiry man named Tito—leaned over from the lower bed.

"Ray talk to you yet?" Tito asked, his voice low.

Kenneth nodded. "Yeah. Gave me some advice about sagging."

Tito smirked. "Good. Ray's been around long enough to know what's what. You're lucky he got to you before someone else did."

Kenneth frowned, the weight of Tito's words adding to the unease already simmering in his chest. "Has that... happened to anyone here?"

Tito's smirk faded, replaced by a grim expression. "More times than you'd think. Some guys come in here thinking they're untouchable. They sag their pants, act tough, try to keep up their street cred. But prison's a whole different game. You send the wrong signal, you pay for it."

Kenneth nodded silently, the reality of his situation settling like a heavy stone in his gut. He had spent so much of his life defining himself through his style, his image, his defiance. Now, those same things felt like liabilities—symbols that could be twisted into something he didn't want to claim.

As the days turned into weeks, Kenneth adjusted to the rhythm of prison life. He kept his jumpsuit pulled tight, his head down, and his focus on surviving. But the lessons he learned here stayed with him, shaping the way he saw himself and the choices he had made.

Sagging wasn't just a fashion statement anymore. It was a reminder of how quickly perceptions could shift—and how dangerous those perceptions could be.

Chapter 16: The Ambush

The sound of water running echoed off the cold, tiled walls of the prison showers. Steam hung in the air, mixing with the sharp scent of soap and mildew. Kenneth stood under the lukewarm spray, his muscles tense despite the relative stillness of the moment. His mind was on Big Ray's warning, his words replaying in a loop: "You send the wrong signal, you pay for it."

Kenneth kept his eyes low, his movements quick and calculated. He scrubbed the soap across his skin, focused on finishing as fast as possible. Around him, the other inmates moved in and out of the showers, some talking in hushed tones, others eyeing their surroundings with the same caution Kenneth felt in his bones.

But the tension in the room was palpable, like the crackle of an approaching storm. Kenneth could feel it—an unease that made his skin crawl.

As he reached for his towel, he caught a glimpse of movement in his peripheral vision. Three men had entered the showers, their faces hard, their postures predatory. Kenneth's heart sank as they spread out, blocking the exit. He recognized one of them—Deebo, a towering figure with scars running down his arms and a reputation for taking what he wanted.

"Yo, new boy," Deebo called, his voice low and menacing. "You in a hurry or something?"

Kenneth froze, his towel gripped tightly in his hands. He glanced around, hoping someone might intervene, but the other inmates had turned their backs, pretending not to notice. This was how it worked in prison—every man for himself.

"I ain't looking for trouble," Kenneth said, his voice steady despite the panic rising in his chest.

Deebo chuckled, a deep, guttural sound. "Trouble? Nah, we just wanna talk. Ain't that right, boys?"

The other two men grinned, their eyes gleaming with malice. Kenneth took a step back, his bare feet slipping slightly on the wet tiles. His mind raced, searching for a way out, but there was none. He was cornered.

The first blow came fast—a punch to his stomach that knocked the wind out of him. Kenneth doubled over, gasping for air, but before he could recover, the second man grabbed him by the shoulders, slamming him against the wall.

"Relax," Deebo said, his tone mocking. "Ain't nobody gonna hear you scream in here."

Kenneth struggled, his fists flailing, but the men were too

strong. They pinned him in place, their laughter ringing in his ears as they tore away his towel. His mind screamed for help, but his voice refused to come. The fear was paralyzing.

What followed was a blur of pain, humiliation, and rage. Kenneth's world narrowed to the cold tiles against his skin, the overpowering stench of sweat, and the sound of his own ragged breathing. Time seemed to stretch, every second an eternity.

The first touch was a violation, a rough hand grabbing his cock. He jerked away, but it was too late. The men had what they wanted. Deebo sneered, his teeth gleaming in the harsh fluorescent light.

"Looks like we got ourselves a new toy, boys," he said, his grip tightening. Kenneth's eyes widened in horror as he felt his body respond despite his desperate attempts to fight it.

The other inmates—his former allies—closed in, their eyes hungry and predatory. They had been waiting for this moment, watching him from the shadows, biding their time. The shower block had been cleared for their sick game, the water running a sadistic serenade to their conquest.

"You like that?" Deebo taunted, stroking Kenneth's erect shaft. Kenneth's eyes rolled back in his head, a whimper escaping his lips. He didn't want to like it, but his body betrayed him. His skin was on fire, his pulse racing, as the hand on his cock grew bolder.

The men took turns, touching him, pinching his nipples, slapping his ass. They whispered vile things in his ear, their breath hot and sticky with lust. Kenneth's thoughts raced, trying to find a way out, trying to understand how he had gotten here.

The prison had been a world unto itself, a place where he thought he could make his mark, a place where he could be someone. But now, naked and vulnerable, he knew the truth. He was nothing but a pawn in a much larger, much dirtier game.

Deebo leaned in, his breath hot and rank. "You're gonna learn to love this, pretty boy. You're gonna beg for it every night."

Kenneth's body was no longer his own. The men touched him, used him, their rough hands and mouths leaving bruises and bite marks. They were insatiable, their desire a living, breathing beast that consumed him whole. He was theirs, their plaything, and there was nothing he could do to stop them.

He felt hands spreading his legs, heard the sound of a zipper being pulled down. He knew what was coming next, and he tried to resist, but his body was limp with fear and arousal. The head of Deebo's cock pressed against his asshole, and then, with one brutal push, he was inside him.

The pain was unbearable, a white-hot agony that made him see stars. He screamed, but the sound was lost in the cacophony of their laughter and the pounding of the shower. He felt himself being torn apart, invaded in the most primal way possible. The other inmates watched with glee, some of them stroking their own penis in anticipation.

Deebo didn't stop, didn't slow down. He fucked Kenneth mercilessly, driving his penis deeper and deeper with every thrust. Kenneth's legs trembled, his knees threatening to give way. He was a ragdoll in the hands of a monster, his body a battleground for their twisted desires.

The next man stepped up, his penis thick and throbbing. Kenneth knew his name—Rico—but the recognition meant nothing now. He was just another face in the crowd, another body to be used and discarded.

Rico didn't bother with pretense. He just took what he wanted, pushing into Kenneth's ass without a moment's hesitation. Kenneth's eyes rolled back in his head, his mouth opening in a silent scream. The pain was unrelenting, a never-ending assault on his senses.

The men took turns, passing him around like a cheap whore. They used his mouth, his butt, his body, and all the while, Kenneth felt himself slipping away, his mind retreating to a place where he couldn't feel the pain, where he couldn't hear the laughter.

He was lost in a sea of sweat and semen, a place where the only things that existed were the men's penis and his own helplessness. His body was no longer his own, a mere receptacle for their desires.
As the last man pulled out, Kenneth slumped to the floor, his body spent and broken. The men laughed, slapping him on the butt and telling him what a good boy he had been. He couldn't even muster the energy to fight them anymore.
He lay there, shivering and sobbing, as they finished their showers and left him, the water running cold and unforgiving. He was alone, his dignity shattered, his soul in tatters.

When it was over, Kenneth lay crumpled on the floor, his body trembling and his mind numb. The men walked away without a word, their laughter fading as they disappeared down the corridor. The other inmates still avoided looking at him, their silence as damning as the assault itself.

Kenneth tried to push himself up, but his limbs refused to cooperate. Pain radiated through his body, sharp and unrelenting, and he realized with a sickening certainty that he couldn't stay here. He needed help.

Two guards found him minutes later, their expressions shifting from indifference to alarm as they took in the scene. One of them radioed for medical assistance while the other crouched beside Kenneth, his voice gruff but not unkind.

"Can you stand?" the guard asked.

Kenneth shook his head, his throat tight with unshed tears. He felt broken—physically, emotionally, completely.

The next few hours passed in a haze. Kenneth was taken to the prison hospital, where a team of medical staff treated his injuries with a detached professionalism that made him feel like an object rather than a person. He avoided their eyes, ashamed and humiliated, the weight of what had happened pressing down on him like a suffocating blanket.

"You're lucky," one of the nurses said as she cleaned a gash on his forehead. "It could've been worse."

Kenneth didn't respond. He couldn't bring himself to speak, the words caught in a whirlwind of shame and anger.

Later, as he lay in the hospital bed, staring at the cracked ceiling tiles, a guard entered the room. It was Big Ray, his expression grim.

"I heard," Ray said, pulling up a chair beside the bed. "Tried to warn you, kid."

Kenneth turned his head away, his jaw clenched. He didn't want to hear it, didn't want to relive the nightmare that had already seared itself into his memory.

Big Ray sighed, leaning forward. "Look, I know you're hurting. But you gotta learn something from this. You can't let these guys see weakness, 'cause they'll use it against you every chance they get."

Kenneth's voice cracked as he finally spoke. "What was I supposed to do? There were three of them."

Ray nodded slowly, his eyes filled with a rare flicker of sympathy. "I get it. Sometimes, there ain't nothing you can do. But you're still here, kid. That means you fight. You heal up, you keep your head down, and you don't give them another reason to come after you."

The days in the hospital blurred together, each one marked by quiet reflection and mounting determination. Kenneth replayed the events over and over, trying to make sense of what had happened, trying to find a way to move forward.

By the time he was transferred to another facility for his safety, Kenneth was no longer the same. The experience had carved something out of him—something raw and fragile, but also something resolute.

He would survive. Somehow, he would find a way to take back the pieces of himself that had been stolen. And he would never forget the lesson he had learned: in this world, every choice carried a cost. And sometimes, that cost was almost too much to bear.

Chapter 17: The Transfer

Kenneth sat on the edge of his hospital bed, staring at the dull linoleum floor beneath his bare feet. The sterile scent of disinfectant filled the air, but he barely noticed. His body ached in ways he hadn't known were possible, but the physical pain was nothing compared to the weight in his chest. Shame, anger, and despair churned together, creating a storm he couldn't escape.

The door to his room creaked open, and a guard stepped in. "Gilbert," he said, his voice brusque. "Pack it up. You're being transferred."

Kenneth glanced up, his expression blank. He had known this was coming—word had spread quickly about what had happened in the shower. For his own safety, the prison administration had decided to move him to another facility. But the knowledge didn't make the reality any easier to accept.

"Yes, sir," Kenneth muttered, his voice hollow. He stood slowly, wincing as the motion sent a sharp pang through his ribs. He gathered the meager belongings he had accumulated during his time in prison—a few books, a small notebook, and a worn pencil—and followed the guard out of the room.

The transport van was cold and cramped, the metal bench digging into Kenneth's back as he sat in silence. The other inmates being transferred avoided his gaze, their faces hard and unreadable. Kenneth kept his head down, focusing on the rhythmic hum of the engine as the van rumbled down the highway.

As the hours passed, he couldn't help but reflect on how far he had fallen. Just months ago, he had been a free man, walking the streets with his jeans sagging low and a swagger in his step. Now, that same choice had become a liability—a symbol that had marked him as prey in a place where survival was the only rule.

Kenneth clenched his fists, his nails digging into his palms. He hated how powerless he felt, how easily his sense of control had been stripped away. But beneath the anger, there was something else—a flicker of determination. He had survived the ambush, survived the hospital, and now, he would survive whatever came next.

The new facility was smaller than the one Kenneth had left, but the atmosphere was no less oppressive. The guards ushered him through intake, handing him a new set of clothes and assigning him to a cell in a quieter wing of the prison. The other inmates in this block seemed older, more subdued, their eyes filled with a wary wisdom that came from years behind bars.

Kenneth's new cellmate was a man in his fifties named Lewis. His graying hair was cropped short, and his weathered face bore the lines of someone who had seen it all. Lewis greeted Kenneth with a nod but didn't press for conversation. Kenneth was grateful for the silence.

That evening, as Kenneth sat on his bunk, Lewis finally spoke. "Word travels fast," he said, his voice low and gravelly. "Heard about what happened to you."

Kenneth stiffened, his jaw tightening. "I don't want to talk about it."

Lewis nodded, leaning back against the wall. "Fair enough. But if you're gonna make it in here, you need to learn something: pride won't keep you safe. It'll get you killed."

Kenneth glanced at him, his eyes narrowing. "What's that supposed to mean?"

"It means you gotta let go of the idea that you're untouchable," Lewis said. "You walk around here thinking you're too tough to be messed with, and someone's gonna prove you wrong. The smart ones keep their heads down, blend in, and wait for their time."

Kenneth didn't respond. He knew Lewis was right, but the words still stung. He had spent so much of his life trying to prove himself—to his mother, to his friends, to himself. Letting go of that felt like admitting defeat.

The days in the new prison passed slowly. Kenneth threw himself into the routine, focusing on work assignments and avoiding unnecessary interactions. He kept his jumpsuit pulled tight, his posture straight, and his eyes forward. He noticed the way the other inmates in his block moved—calculated and deliberate, like predators circling prey. He made a point of staying out of their way.

But the nightmares didn't stop. Every night, Kenneth relived the ambush, the laughter of his attackers echoing in his ears.

He woke up in a cold sweat, his heart racing, and spent hours staring at the ceiling, unable to fall back asleep.

One afternoon, during recreation time, Kenneth found himself sitting alone on a bench in the yard. He watched as the other inmates milled about, their movements purposeful and restrained. The air was thick with unspoken rules, and Kenneth was beginning to understand them.

Lewis approached, a cigarette dangling from his lips. He sat down beside Kenneth without a word, the two of them watching the yard in silence.

"You ever think about what you'll do when you get out?" Lewis asked finally.

Kenneth frowned, the question catching him off guard. "I don't know," he admitted. "Feels like forever away."

Lewis nodded, exhaling a plume of smoke. "It does. But it's not. Time keeps moving, whether you like it or not. The question is, what are you gonna do with it?"

Kenneth didn't have an answer. He had spent so much of his time in prison just trying to survive, he hadn't allowed himself to think about what came next. But Lewis's words lingered in his mind, planting a seed of possibility.

That night, as Kenneth lay in his bunk, he pulled out the small notebook he had brought with him. The pages were blank, save for a few scribbles from his first days in prison. He picked up the pencil and began to write, the words coming slowly at first but gaining momentum as his thoughts poured onto the page.

He wrote about the ambush, about Big Ray's warning, about the shame and anger that still gnawed at him. But he also wrote about the flicker of determination he felt—the stubborn refusal to let this place break him.

By the time he set the notebook aside, the weight in his chest felt just a little lighter. He didn't have all the answers yet, but for the first time in weeks, he felt like he was moving forward.

Chapter 18: The Release

The gate clanged shut behind him, the sound reverberating through Kenneth's chest like a bell signaling the end of a long, punishing sentence. He stood there for a moment, frozen, staring out at the world beyond the prison walls. The air smelled different—fresher, freer—but it felt strange to him now, foreign in a way that made his stomach twist.

"Gilbert!" a voice called, snapping him out of his thoughts. A corrections officer stood nearby, holding a manila envelope. "Here's your release paperwork and your belongings."

Kenneth walked over, taking the envelope. Inside was a faded ID, the cash he had on him the day of his arrest, and a piece of paper listing his parole conditions. The officer handed him a bag containing the clothes he'd been wearing when he was arrested—jeans and a hoodie that now felt like relics from another life.

As Kenneth pulled on the familiar hoodie, his hands brushed against the jeans, the fabric soft and worn from years of use. He hesitated for a moment, then shoved them into the bag. He had no desire to wear them now, not after everything they had come to symbolize.

The officer gave him one last look, his expression unreadable. "Good luck out there," he said curtly, before turning back toward the gate.

Kenneth nodded mutely, the words feeling hollow. He slung the bag over his shoulder and started walking toward the parking lot, his heart heavy with uncertainty.

Carla was waiting for him outside, her car parked at the curb. Kenneth's chest tightened when he saw her, a rush of emotions flooding through him—relief, shame, gratitude. She stepped out of the car, her face lighting up with a smile that didn't quite hide the tears in her eyes.

"Come here, baby," she said, opening her arms.

Kenneth hesitated, then stepped forward, letting her pull him into a hug. Her embrace was warm and familiar, and for the first time in years, he felt a small measure of comfort.

"I'm so glad you're out," she whispered, pulling back to look at him. "We're gonna get you back on your feet. One step at a time."

Kenneth nodded, his throat too tight to speak. He climbed into the car, setting the bag of clothes at his feet, and stared out the window as they drove away from the prison. The world outside seemed sharper, louder than he remembered, and the weight of his release pressed down on him like a physical thing.

The first few days home were surreal. Carla had cleaned and redecorated his old room, painting the walls a calming blue and replacing the tattered posters with framed photographs of their family. Kenneth appreciated her effort, but the room felt unfamiliar, like it belonged to someone else.

Carla hovered, her concern evident in every gesture. She cooked his favorite meals, reminded him to take things slow, and tried her best to fill the silence with warmth. But Kenneth found it hard to talk. His words felt heavy, tangled with emotions he didn't know how to express.

One evening, Carla brought him a box of old photographs. "I thought these might make your room feel more like home," she said, setting it on his desk. "Take your time going through them."

Kenneth waited until she left before opening the box. Inside were pictures of his childhood—birthdays, holidays, and candid moments he barely remembered. At the bottom of the pile was a photo of him at sixteen, wearing his favorite sagging jeans and a wide grin. He stared at it for a long time, the image stirring a mix of nostalgia and regret.

A week later, Carla sat him down at the kitchen table, a flyer in her hand. "There's a job opening at Mr. Harris's farm," she said. "He's looking for help with the crops. It's hard work, but it's honest, and he's willing to give you a chance."

Kenneth took the flyer, studying the address printed at the bottom. The idea of working on a farm felt foreign, but he could see the hope in Carla's eyes. He didn't want to disappoint her—not again.

"I'll give him a call," Kenneth said quietly.

The farm was sprawling, its fields stretching out to the horizon. Kenneth arrived early on his first day, nervous but determined. Mr. Harris, a gruff man in his sixties with a weathered face, greeted him with a firm handshake.

"Your mama vouched for you," Mr. Harris said. "Said you're looking to turn things around. That true?"

"Yes, sir," Kenneth replied, meeting the man's gaze.

"Good," Harris said, nodding. "You do your job, you'll have no trouble from me."

The work was grueling—long hours spent planting, weeding, and harvesting under the hot sun. Kenneth's muscles ached at the end of each day, but the physical exhaustion was a welcome distraction from the thoughts that still haunted him. He found a strange solace in the rhythm of the work, a sense of purpose in the tangible results of his efforts.

One evening, as Kenneth sat on the porch after dinner, Carla joined him, handing him a glass of sweet tea. They sat in companionable silence for a while, watching the sun dip below the horizon.

"I'm proud of you, Kenneth," Carla said finally. "I know it hasn't been easy, but you're doing it. You're moving forward."

Kenneth looked down at his hands, rough and calloused from the farm work. "Sometimes it doesn't feel like enough," he admitted. "Like I'll never get past what happened."

Carla reached over, placing a hand on his. "You can't change the past, baby. But you can decide what you do with your future. And I see a good man in you—a man who's learning and growing."

Kenneth swallowed hard, nodding. "Thanks, Ma."

Over time, Kenneth began to feel a sense of stability returning to his life. He worked hard on the farm, saved his money, and even started attending a support group for former inmates. The group was small but welcoming, and for the first time, Kenneth felt like he wasn't alone in his struggles.

One evening, after a particularly long day in the fields, Kenneth sat down with his notebook. He flipped through the pages, reading the words he had written during his darkest moments in prison. They were raw and painful, but they were also a testament to how far he had come.

He picked up his pen and began to write again, this time about the life he was building—a life defined not by his mistakes, but by the lessons he had learned from them.

Chapter 19: The Reflection

The morning sun streamed through the curtains of Kenneth's room, casting long, warm streaks of light across the wooden floor. He sat at the small desk Carla had given him, his notebook open in front of him, a pen resting loosely in his fingers. The pages were filled with his thoughts—raw and unfiltered—spanning his journey from the carefree teenager who once walked the school halls with his jeans sagging low to the man he was becoming.

Kenneth leaned back in his chair, letting his gaze drift to the framed photographs on the wall. His mother had chosen them carefully: family gatherings, childhood memories, and one of Kenneth as a baby, his chubby face lit up with a toothless grin. That innocence seemed a lifetime away.

The journey that brought him here had been anything but linear. There were moments of clarity, like the first time he planted a seed on the Harris farm and realized how much patience and care it took to make something grow. And there were moments of deep despair, like the nights in his cell when the weight of his choices threatened to crush him.

Kenneth picked up the pen and began to write.

"The boy I was couldn't see this coming," he began. "He thought the world revolved around respect—earning it, demanding it. Sagging my jeans was my way of showing the world I didn't care what it thought of me. But it wasn't confidence. It was armor. A flimsy shield I thought would protect me from judgment, from fear, from everything I didn't want to face. It never did."

The words flowed easily now, his pen gliding across the page.

"I blamed everyone else for a long time. The kids at school who teased me. The men who whistled or whispered as I walked by. The cops who arrested me, the system that locked me up. But the truth is, I made my choices. And those choices led me exactly where I didn't want to go."

Kenneth set the pen down, his hand cramping slightly from the effort. He glanced out the window at the Harris farm, where the fields stretched out under the morning sky. The work there was honest, tiring, and grounding. It gave him a sense of control over his life—something he hadn't felt in years.

It was Mr. Harris who had taught him the value of patience.

"You don't plant a seed today and expect fruit tomorrow," Harris had said one afternoon as they worked side by side in the heat. "Takes time. Takes care. And sometimes, even when you do everything right, the crop still fails. That's life. But you get back up and try again."

Those words had stayed with Kenneth, replaying in his mind as he worked long days in the fields and wrote long nights at his desk.

Later that morning, Carla joined him in the kitchen, a plate of toast and eggs in her hands. She sat down across from him, her eyes filled with quiet pride as she watched him sip his coffee.

"You've been writing a lot lately," she said, her tone light but curious.

Kenneth nodded. “Yeah. It helps me make sense of things.”

Carla smiled softly. “I always knew you had a good head on your shoulders. Just took you a while to use it.”

Kenneth chuckled, the sound dry but genuine. “Yeah. Guess I had to learn the hard way.”

Carla reached across the table, placing her hand over his. “I’m proud of you, Kenneth. Not just for what you’ve been through, but for what you’re doing now. You’re building something—something real. That takes courage.”

Kenneth swallowed hard, her words sinking deep. “Thanks, Ma. I’m trying.”

After breakfast, Kenneth decided to take a walk through the fields. The farm was quiet this time of day, the air cool and fragrant with the smell of freshly turned soil. He let his thoughts wander as he walked, his steps steady and unhurried.

He thought about Big Ray, the older inmate who had given him his first real warning in prison. Ray’s words about survival had been blunt, even brutal, but they had kept Kenneth alive. He owed a lot to the man who had seen something in him worth protecting.

He thought about Lewis, his second cellmate, who had shown him that survival wasn’t just about keeping your head down—it was about planning for what came next. Lewis had taught Kenneth the importance of looking beyond the prison walls, of imagining a life after confinement.

And he thought about J-Roc, the man who had drawn him into

the world of fast money and dangerous decisions. Kenneth's feelings about J-Roc were complicated. There was anger, yes, but also a strange gratitude. Without J-Roc, Kenneth might never have learned how quickly the allure of easy money could turn into a trap.

As Kenneth walked, he found himself nearing the edge of the farm, where a row of oak trees stood tall and resolute. He stopped beneath one of the larger trees, leaning against its sturdy trunk. The shade was cool, the breeze gentle, and for a moment, Kenneth closed his eyes, letting the sounds of the farm wash over him.

This was peace, he realized—not the absence of struggle, but the presence of purpose. For so long, he had searched for meaning in rebellion, in image, in the approval of others. Now, he found it in the simple act of working the land, of creating something tangible and lasting.

When Kenneth returned to the house, he found Carla sitting on the porch with two glasses of lemonade. She handed him one as he sat beside her, the cool drink refreshing after his walk.

"You've come a long way," Carla said, her voice soft.

Kenneth nodded, his gaze fixed on the horizon. "Feels like a lifetime ago. Everything that happened."

Carla placed a hand on his arm. "But it's not just about what happened. It's about what you do with it. You've got a second chance, Kenneth. Not everyone gets that."

Kenneth looked at her, his eyes reflecting the gratitude he felt but couldn't quite put into words. "I won't waste it," he said finally. "I promise."

That evening, Kenneth sat down at his desk again, his notebook open to a fresh page. He thought about the lessons he had learned—the hard truths about identity, choices, and consequences. He thought about the man he wanted to be for his future family, for himself.

He began to write.

"The sagging pants were just a symbol. I didn't see it then, but I see it now. They represented everything I thought I wanted—freedom, confidence, power. But they also hid everything I was afraid of—vulnerability, uncertainty, and the fear of being judged. I don't sag anymore, not because someone told me to stop, but because I don't need them to tell my story. I tell it myself, now."

The words poured out of him, each one a step forward, a brick in the foundation he was building for his new life.

Chapter 20: The New Beginning

The sun was rising over the Harris farm, painting the fields in hues of gold and amber. Kenneth stood at the edge of the porch, a steaming cup of coffee in his hand, watching as the first light of day broke across the horizon. The air was crisp, carrying the faint scent of soil and dew. It was a quiet morning, the kind Kenneth had come to cherish. Each day was a gift now, a chance to rebuild.

After months of working on the farm, Kenneth had found a rhythm that gave him a sense of purpose. His muscles were lean and strong, his hands roughened by hard labor, and his mind clearer than it had been in years. But it wasn't just the work that grounded him—it was the community that surrounded him.

Mr. Harris had become a mentor, teaching Kenneth not just the skills of farming but also the values of perseverance and accountability. Carla had been his rock, her unwavering support guiding him through the toughest moments of his transition. And the support group he attended weekly had given him a safe space to share his struggles and listen to the stories of others who had walked similar paths.

One afternoon, as Kenneth was loading bales of hay onto the truck, Mr. Harris approached him, wiping sweat from his brow.

"You've done good here, Kenneth," Harris said, his voice gruff but kind. "I know this work ain't easy, but you've stuck with it. That says a lot."

Kenneth set down the bale, turning to face the older man. "Thanks, Mr. Harris. It's been good for me. Feels like I'm finally doing something that matters."

Harris nodded, a hint of pride in his eyes. "You're not just working the land, son. You're working on yourself. And that's the hardest job there is."

Kenneth smiled, the words settling in his chest like a warm ember.

Later that week, Kenneth sat down with Carla at the kitchen table, a stack of papers spread out in front of him. They were applications—job opportunities, training programs, and even a community college course catalog.

"You've got options now," Carla said, her tone encouraging. "You've worked hard to get to this point, and I'm proud of you. But it's time to think about what's next."

Kenneth nodded, his gaze focused on the papers. He hadn't thought much about the future beyond the farm, but Carla was right—it was time to start planning. He picked up one of the applications, scanning the details of a welding certification program.

"This one looks good," he said, tapping the paper. "It's hands-on, and it's something I could see myself doing long-term."

Carla smiled. "Then go for it. You've got the drive, Kenneth. You just need to take the next step."

The weeks that followed were a whirlwind of preparation. Kenneth balanced his farm duties with studying for the entrance exam and completing the necessary paperwork for the welding program. It was challenging, but he embraced the process, driven by the desire to build a stable future.

On the day of his exam, Carla drove him to the testing center. As they pulled into the parking lot, she placed a hand on his arm.

"No matter what happens today, I'm proud of you," she said. "You've already come so far."

Kenneth nodded, taking a deep breath. "Thanks, Ma. I'll do my best."

The test was harder than Kenneth had expected, the questions demanding both precision and critical thinking. But he stayed focused, drawing on the discipline he had developed over the past months. By the time he handed in his paper, he felt a mix of exhaustion and cautious optimism.

Two weeks later, Kenneth received a letter in the mail. He stood on the porch, the envelope trembling slightly in his hands as he opened it. Carla watched from the doorway, her expression anxious but hopeful.

As Kenneth read the words, a smile spread across his face. "I got in," he said, his voice filled with disbelief and joy. "I got in."

Carla rushed forward, pulling him into a tight hug. "I knew you would," she said, her voice thick with emotion. "I'm so proud of you, Kenneth."

The welding program was intense, requiring long hours of study and practice. But Kenneth thrived in the structured environment, his hands steady as he learned to shape and fuse metal. His instructors recognized his potential, often praising his attention to detail and work ethic.

For the first time in his life, Kenneth felt like he was building something tangible—both in his work and in himself.

By the time Kenneth completed the program, he had not only earned his certification but also secured a job at a local manufacturing plant. The position paid well, and the sense of independence it offered was deeply satisfying.

On his first day at the plant, Kenneth arrived early, dressed in his new uniform and carrying a lunchbox Carla had packed for him. As he stepped onto the factory floor, he felt a surge of pride. This was his chance to create a stable life, to prove to himself and to those who believed in him that he could succeed.

That evening, Kenneth sat on the porch with Carla, a quiet sense of accomplishment settling over him. The road ahead wasn't without challenges, but for the first time, he felt ready to face them.

"You've built a good life, Kenneth," Carla said, her voice filled with warmth. "And it's only going to get better."

Kenneth nodded, his gaze fixed on the horizon. "Yeah. It is."

As the sun dipped below the horizon, Kenneth picked up his

notebook, flipping to a fresh page. He began to write, his words filled with hope and determination.

“This is my new beginning. It’s not perfect, and it’s not easy. But it’s mine. And that’s enough.”

Chapter 21: The Sagging Situation

The late afternoon sun cast a warm glow over the neighborhood park, where Kenneth stood watching his two sons, Devin and Malachi, chase each other across the grass. Their laughter carried on the breeze, a reminder of how far Kenneth had come. Carla sat on a nearby bench, chatting with a neighbor, her face lit with an easy smile.

Kenneth adjusted his jeans, which now fit snugly at his waist—a far cry from the sagging pants he used to wear. It was a conscious choice, one he had committed to years ago after realizing the impact of his appearance on how he was perceived and how he felt about himself. The sagging pants had been part of a younger, less mature version of Kenneth—one who had mistaken rebellion for identity.

A group of teens loitered near the basketball court, their loud banter catching Kenneth’s attention. One of the boys had his pants sagging so low that his entire waistband of bright blue underwear was visible. Kenneth couldn’t help but shake his head. The sight sparked a flood of memories, not all of them pleasant.

He thought back to the days when sagging had been his trademark, a statement of defiance. At the time, he had convinced himself it was just fashion, a harmless way to express himself. But as he matured, he had come to see it differently. The sagging wasn't just uncomfortable for others to look at—it was unprofessional, a distraction from who he truly was, and a barrier to the man he wanted to become.

That evening, after dinner, Kenneth called Devin and Malachi into the living room. They were 12 and 10, full of energy, always eager to listen when their father spoke.

"Hey, boys, let's sit for a bit," Kenneth said, gesturing toward the couch. "I want to talk to you about something."

The boys exchanged curious looks and plopped down on the cushions. Kenneth sat across from them, leaning forward with his elbows on his knees.

"I've been watching you grow up, and I couldn't be prouder of the young men you're becoming," Kenneth began. "But there's something I want you to think about as you get older—the way you present yourselves to the world."

Devin tilted his head. "You mean, like, how we dress?"

Kenneth nodded. "Exactly. When I was your age, I used to sag my pants. I thought it made me look cool, like I didn't care what anyone thought. But what I didn't realize was how uncomfortable it made other people—how it made me look unprofessional, and how it sent the wrong message."

Malachi furrowed his brow. "What kind of message?"

Kenneth hesitated for a moment, choosing his words carefully. "When you sag your pants, people might think you don't take yourself seriously. They might see you as disrespectful or immature. And for some people, it sends a message that you're not being your best self."

Devin leaned forward, his interest piqued. "What do you mean by ‘best self’?”

Kenneth smiled, glad they were engaged. “Being your best self means showing the world you respect yourself and others. It means dressing in a way that reflects who you are—not just what’s popular or easy. When I sagged my pants, I wasn’t thinking about the bigger picture. I wasn’t thinking about how it could be seen as unprofessional, or even how it could send mixed messages to the gay community, who might interpret it in ways I never intended.”

Malachi’s eyes widened. “You mean, like, people thought you were...?”

Kenneth nodded gently. “Exactly. And there’s nothing wrong with people being who they are. But when you’re sending a message you don’t mean to send, it creates confusion. I realized that my choices didn’t reflect who I really was. And more importantly, they didn’t reflect who I wanted to be.”

The boys listened quietly as Kenneth shared more of his story, talking about how he had learned to take pride in his appearance—not for superficial reasons, but because it was part of respecting himself and others.

“Life is about choices,” Kenneth said, his voice steady. “And the way you dress is one of those choices. It’s a small thing, but it matters. It shows the world who you are and what you stand for. I want you both to think about that as you grow up.”

Devin and Malachi nodded, their expressions thoughtful. Kenneth could see the wheels turning in their minds, and he felt a surge of hope. He didn’t expect them to understand everything right away, but planting the seed was enough for now.

Later that night, Kenneth sat at his desk, his notebook open to a blank page. He picked up his pen and began to write.

"The sagging pants were never just about fashion. They were about identity, about trying to fit in, about rebellion. But as I grew, I realized they were also a symbol of holding myself back. Sagging sent messages I didn't mean to send—to others and to myself. It was uncomfortable for people to see, and it wasn't the best version of me. Now, I know better. And I want my sons to know better too."

The next weekend, Kenneth took Devin and Malachi to the Harris farm. The new owners had allowed him to show his boys the fields where he had worked, the place where he had learned the value of hard work and patience.

As they walked through the rows of crops, Kenneth pointed out the tools and explained how much effort it took to nurture the land.

"This is where I learned what it means to take pride in what you do," Kenneth said. "And that lesson applies to everything—not just work, but how you carry yourself, how you treat people, and how you present yourself."

Malachi touched the leaves of a corn stalk, his eyes wide with wonder. "Is that why you don't sag your pants anymore?"

Kenneth chuckled, ruffling his son's hair. "Exactly. Because I want to be the best version of myself. And I want you two to be the best versions of yourselves too."

As they drove home, Kenneth felt a deep sense of peace. He had made mistakes, but he had also learned from them. And now, he was passing those lessons down to his sons, ensuring they had the tools to make better choices.

Later that night, as the boys slept and Carla read a book

beside him, Kenneth reflected on how far he had come. The sagging pants were long gone, but their lesson remained—a reminder of how small changes could lead to big transformations.

As he drifted off to sleep, Kenneth thought about the future—not just his own, but his family's. He had made his peace with the past, and now, he was focused on building a legacy rooted in respect, responsibility, and growth.

Chapter 22: The Impact

Kenneth stood in front of his small congregation of family and friends, gathered at the community center for a local mentorship program. The space was modest, with folding chairs arranged in neat rows and a lectern set up at the front. It wasn't a large crowd, but it was meaningful—a mix of young men from the neighborhood, their parents, and a few mentors like Kenneth who had volunteered to share their experiences.

The program's organizer, a retired schoolteacher named Mrs. Jenkins, introduced Kenneth with a warm smile. "This young man has a powerful story to share. He's walked a hard road, but he's come out stronger on the other side. Let's give a big welcome to Mr. Kenneth Gilbert."

The audience clapped politely, and Kenneth approached the lectern, his heart pounding in his chest. He had spoken in small groups before, but this was different. This was his chance to make a difference, to share the lessons he had learned with others who might be walking a similar path.

Kenneth took a deep breath, his hands gripping the edges of the lectern. "Thank you, Mrs. Jenkins, and thank you all for being here today. I'm not going to stand here and pretend I've got it all figured out, but I do want to share something I've learned—something I wish I'd understood sooner."

He paused, letting his gaze sweep across the room. Many of the young men in the audience were dressed like he used to be—baggy jeans, hoodies, sneakers. He saw pieces of his younger self in them, and it stirred a deep sense of responsibility.

"When I was younger," he began, "I thought the way I dressed was just fashion. I thought it made me look cool, made me feel confident. But the truth is, it didn't. It wasn't about confidence—it was about hiding. I used sagging pants as a way to say, 'I don't care what you think,' but deep down, I cared a lot."

The room was silent, the audience hanging on his every word. Kenneth continued, his voice steady.

"What I didn't realize back then was that the way you present yourself matters. It's not just about how other people see you—it's about how you see yourself. When I sagged my pants, I wasn't sending the message I thought I was. Instead, I was telling the world that I didn't take myself seriously. I was telling myself the same thing."

A hand went up in the back row, and Kenneth nodded toward the young man who had raised it. "Go ahead."

The boy stood, his voice hesitant but curious. "So... are you saying the way we dress can, like, change how we feel about ourselves?"

Kenneth smiled, glad for the question. "Exactly. It's about respect—respect for yourself and for the people around you. When I stopped sagging my pants, it wasn't just a fashion choice. It was a decision to be the best version of myself, to show the world that I was serious about my future."

The questions kept coming, and Kenneth answered each one thoughtfully. He spoke about his experiences in prison, the lessons he had learned, and the choices he had made to turn his life around. But he also emphasized that it wasn't just about clothes—it was about mindset.

"Don't get me wrong," he said. "Changing the way I dressed didn't fix everything. It was just one step in a bigger process. But it was an important step. It helped me see myself differently, and it helped other people see me differently too."

After the session ended, several young men approached Kenneth, their faces filled with a mix of admiration and curiosity. One of them, a lanky teenager named Marcus, lingered behind, waiting until the others had left before speaking.

"Mr. Gilbert," Marcus said, his voice low, "I just wanted to say... thanks. What you said really hit me. I've been... trying to figure some stuff out, you know? And it helps to hear someone who's been through it."

Kenneth nodded, his expression warm. "I get it, Marcus. And I'm glad you're thinking about this now. You've got a whole future ahead of you. Make choices that'll help you get where you want to go."

Marcus nodded, a small smile breaking across his face. "Thanks. I will."

Later that evening, Kenneth sat on the porch with Carla, the two of them enjoying the cool breeze as the stars began to emerge. He told her about the mentorship session, about the questions the boys had asked and the conversations it had sparked.

"You're making a real difference, Kenneth," Carla said, her

voice filled with pride. "I hope you see that."

Kenneth nodded, his gaze fixed on the horizon. "I do. And I hope they do too. It's not easy to change, but if I can help even one of them avoid the mistakes I made, it's worth it."

Carla leaned her head against his shoulder, her presence a steady comfort. "You're building something beautiful, Kenneth—not just for yourself, but for all of us."

As the night deepened, Kenneth returned to his desk, his notebook waiting for him. He opened it to a fresh page and began to write.

"The impact of our choices goes beyond ourselves. It ripples out, touching the lives of the people around us. When I stopped sagging my pants, it wasn't just about me. It was about the man I wanted to be, the father I wanted to become, and the example I wanted to set. Today, I see those ripples in my sons, in the young men I mentor, and in the community I'm part of. The impact is real. And it's worth it."

Chapter 23: The Message

The community center was bustling with activity as Kenneth entered, a leather-bound notebook tucked under his arm. The annual youth outreach event had drawn a larger crowd than expected, with teenagers and parents filling every corner of the hall. Posters with motivational quotes and photos of local mentors adorned the walls, each one bearing the tagline: "Change Starts With You."

Kenneth adjusted his collar, feeling a mix of nerves and excitement. He had been invited to speak as the event's keynote speaker—a role he hadn't anticipated when he first started mentoring. But as he looked around the room at the young faces, some curious, others guarded, he felt a deep sense of purpose. This wasn't just about him anymore. This was about the message.

As the program began, Kenneth listened to the other speakers, nodding along to their stories of struggle and triumph. Finally, it was his turn. The applause was warm but subdued as he walked to the podium. He set his notebook down, resting his hands on either side of the lectern.

"Thank you all for being here today," he began, his voice steady. "It means a lot to see so many young people and their families coming together to talk about change, about growth, and about the choices we make every day."

He paused, letting his gaze sweep across the audience. "When I was your age, I didn't think much about my choices. I thought I had time, that the things I did didn't matter in the grand scheme of things. But I was wrong. Every choice matters—big or small. And sometimes, the smallest choices can have the biggest impact."

Kenneth took a deep breath, glancing briefly at his notebook before continuing. "For me, it started with something as simple as how I wore my pants. I know that might sound trivial, but it wasn't. Back then, I sagged my pants because it was the style. It was what my friends did, what I saw in music videos. But what I didn't realize was that it sent a message—a message I didn't even mean to send."

He leaned forward slightly, his tone earnest. "It was uncomfortable for people to look at. It was unprofessional. And more than that, it said something about me that wasn't true. It made people think I didn't care about myself, about my future. And for some, it sent a message to the gay community, one I never intended to send. It wasn't who I was. But it was who I let the world see."

The audience was silent, their attention focused entirely on Kenneth. He let the weight of his words settle before continuing.

"Changing the way I dressed was one of the first steps I took toward becoming the man I wanted to be. It wasn't about following rules or conforming—it was about respect. Respect for myself and for the people around me. When I pulled up my pants, I wasn't just changing my appearance. I was changing my mindset."

A young girl in the front row raised her hand hesitantly. Kenneth gestured for her to speak. "But, like, does how you dress really matter that much?" she asked, her voice tinged with skepticism.

Kenneth smiled warmly. "That's a great question. And the answer is yes, it does. It's not about impressing people or fitting in—it's about the message you send, to others and to yourself. When you take pride in how you present yourself, you're saying, 'I take myself seriously. I value who I am and where I'm going.' And that message matters."

As the session continued, Kenneth shared more of his story, from the choices that led him to prison to the mentors who had helped him find his way back. He talked about the power of small changes, of surrounding yourself with people who lift you up, and of taking responsibility for your life.

"I'm not saying it's easy," he said. "It's not. But every step you take in the right direction brings you closer to the life you want. And it starts with a decision—one decision, every day, to be better than you were yesterday."

After his speech, Kenneth was surrounded by young people asking questions, sharing their own struggles, and seeking advice. One boy, no older than 16, approached him hesitantly.

"Mr. Gilbert," the boy said, his voice barely above a whisper, "do you really think I can change? Even if... even if I've already messed up?"

Kenneth placed a reassuring hand on the boy's shoulder. "Absolutely," he said firmly. "We've all messed up. What matters is what you do next. It's never too late to start making better choices."

The boy nodded, a glimmer of hope in his eyes. "Thanks," he said quietly.

That evening, as Kenneth packed up his things, Mrs. Jenkins approached him, her face glowing with pride.

"You've got a gift, Kenneth," she said. "The way you connect with these kids—it's something special. I hope you keep sharing your message. They need to hear it."

Kenneth smiled, humbled by her words. "Thank you, Mrs. Jenkins. It means a lot to me."

At home, Kenneth sat down at his desk, his notebook open in front of him. He thought about the event, the young faces in the crowd, and the questions they had asked. Picking up his pen, he began to write.

"The message isn't just about sagging pants. It's about the choices we make, the respect we show ourselves, and the futures we build. Changing the way I dressed was just the beginning. The real change came when I started to see myself differently, when I realized I could be more. And that's the message I want to share: we can all be more. We just have to start."

Chapter 24: The Hope

Kenneth sat on the front steps of his house, watching the sunrise paint the sky in soft hues of orange and pink. The morning was still, the kind of quiet that allowed his thoughts to wander freely. In the distance, he could hear the faint sounds of birds waking up and the occasional bark of a neighbor's dog. Carla was still asleep, and his boys were tucked in their beds. For Kenneth, these moments of solitude were precious—a chance to reflect on how far he had come and where he still wanted to go.

Later that morning, Kenneth and Carla loaded the boys into the car for a trip to the local community farm. It was a sunny day, the air crisp and filled with the scent of fresh soil and budding crops. The farm had become a special place for their family, a symbol of growth and renewal. As the car rolled down the gravel driveway, Kenneth glanced in the rearview mirror, catching a glimpse of Devin and Malachi chatting animatedly in the back seat.

"Alright, boys," Kenneth said, his tone playful. "Today's lesson is about hope."

Devin tilted his head, a curious expression on his face. "Hope? Like wishing for something?"

Kenneth smiled. "Not exactly. Hope is about believing in something better, even when things aren't perfect. It's about taking steps toward that better thing, no matter how small they seem."

At the farm, Kenneth led his family through the rows of crops, pointing out the stages of growth in the plants. "See these seeds?" he said, kneeling down to show them a freshly planted row. "When you put them in the ground, you don't see anything right away. But you keep watering them, keep tending to them, and eventually, they grow into something amazing."

Malachi crouched beside him, his small hands brushing the soil. "So, it's like having hope that they'll grow?"

"Exactly," Kenneth said, ruffling Malachi's hair. "And it's the same with life. You might not see the results of your hard work right away, but if you keep going, keep believing, good things will happen."

As the day went on, Kenneth reflected on the lessons he had learned and how they had shaped his view of hope. It wasn't just an abstract concept for him—it was a lifeline. Hope had carried him through the darkest times, through prison walls and self-doubt, and into the light of the life he was building now.

He thought about the mentors who had believed in him when he couldn't believe in himself, about the choices he had made to pull himself out of the cycle of despair. Hope had been the foundation of it all, and he wanted to pass that gift on to his boys.

That evening, after dinner, Kenneth gathered his family in the living room. The fire crackled softly in the hearth, casting a warm glow over the room. Devin and Malachi sat cross-legged on the floor, their eyes wide with anticipation.

"I want to tell you both a story," Kenneth said, leaning forward in his chair. "It's about a man who made a lot of mistakes but decided to change his life."

Devin's brow furrowed. "Is it about you, Dad?"

Kenneth chuckled. "It could be. But it's also about everyone who decides to start over. This man realized that he couldn't change the past, but he could learn from it. He could plant new seeds, seeds of hope, and grow a better future."

Malachi tilted his head. "Did he do it?"

Kenneth nodded, his gaze steady. "He did. But it wasn't easy. It took time and hard work. And most of all, it took hope. He had to believe that things could get better, even when it was hard to see how."

As the boys asked questions and shared their thoughts, Kenneth felt a deep sense of fulfillment. He wasn't just teaching them about hope—he was showing them what it looked like in action. It was in the way he treated Carla, the way he worked hard every day, and the way he carried himself with dignity and respect.

Later that night, Kenneth sat at his desk, his notebook open to a blank page. The words came to him easily, each one a reflection of the hope he had found and the hope he wanted to inspire in others.

"Hope isn't just a feeling. It's a choice. It's the decision to believe in something better, to keep going when things are hard, to plant seeds even when the ground seems barren. Hope is what carried me through the darkest times, and it's what I want to pass on to my sons. Because as long as we have hope, we have a future worth building."

Chapter 25: A New Dawn

Kenneth awoke to the faint sounds of birds chirping outside his window. The soft light of dawn seeped into the room, casting long shadows across the walls. He lay still for a moment, savoring the peace that came with the early hours.

Today was significant—not because of any event or milestone, but because it marked the culmination of a journey he had never thought he'd be strong enough to take.

The morning started as most did. Kenneth helped Carla prepare breakfast while Devin and Malachi set the table. They worked together in a comfortable rhythm, the kind that came from years of shared routines. Kenneth glanced at his sons as they laughed over some inside joke, their easy camaraderie filling the room with warmth. This was the life he had worked so hard to rebuild—a life filled with love, purpose, and the promise of a better future.

After breakfast, Kenneth decided to visit the Harris farm. It had become a sanctuary for him over the years, a place where he could reflect and find clarity. As he drove down the familiar dirt road, memories of his time working the fields flooded his mind. The lessons he had learned there—about patience, resilience, and the power of small beginnings—had shaped him in ways he hadn't realized at the time.

When he arrived, he was greeted by the new owners, a young couple who had taken over after Mr. Harris retired. They welcomed him warmly, inviting him to walk the fields at his leisure. Kenneth wandered through the rows of crops, his hands brushing the leaves as he passed. The farm looked different now, but its essence remained the same: a testament to what could be achieved through dedication and care.

Kenneth found a spot beneath the large oak tree at the edge of the property and sat down, his back against the sturdy trunk. From this vantage point, he could see the entire farm, the neat rows of crops stretching out to the horizon. He pulled out his notebook, the pages filled with his thoughts, lessons, and reflections from over the years. Today, he intended to write his final entry.

"This journey has been about more than just redemption. It's been about transformation—about becoming the man I was always meant to be. I used to think my mistakes defined me, that they were the sum total of who I was. But I've learned that it's not our mistakes that define us—it's how we rise after falling."

Kenneth paused, letting the words sink in before continuing.

"I've been blessed with a second chance, a chance to rebuild my life and to guide my sons toward better choices. They are my legacy, the proof that change is possible, and that hope is never wasted. Through them, I see the future—a future I once thought I didn't deserve."

As he finished writing, Kenneth felt a sense of closure, a deep-seated peace he hadn't experienced before. He closed the notebook and leaned back against the tree, his gaze fixed on the endless sky above. The farm had once been a place of labor, a source of physical and emotional strain. Now, it was a symbol of growth, of everything he had worked so hard to cultivate.

When Kenneth returned home, Carla was waiting for him on the porch. She held two mugs of coffee, the steam rising into the crisp afternoon air. She handed him a mug as he joined her, and they sat side by side, the silence between them comfortable.

"You went to the farm?" Carla asked, breaking the quiet.

Kenneth nodded. "Yeah. Wanted to clear my head. Write some things down."

Carla smiled knowingly. "That place has always been good for you."

"It has," Kenneth agreed. He took a sip of his coffee, savoring the warmth. "I was thinking about everything—about where we started and where we are now. It feels... surreal, sometimes."

Carla reached over, placing a hand on his arm. "You've come so far, Kenneth. We've come so far. And it's all because you chose to change."

Kenneth met her gaze, his heart swelling with gratitude. "I couldn't have done it without you, Carla. You believed in me when I didn't believe in myself. That made all the difference."

That evening, Kenneth called Devin and Malachi into the living room. He had been preparing for this moment for weeks, carefully considering the words he wanted to say. The boys sat on the couch, their expressions curious.

"I wanted to talk to you both about something important," Kenneth began. "About our family, and about the kind of men I hope you'll grow up to be."

Devin tilted his head. "What do you mean, Dad?"

Kenneth smiled, his tone gentle but firm. "I mean being men of character. Men who respect themselves and others. Men who take responsibility for their actions and strive to make the world better, even in small ways."

Malachi leaned forward, his eyes wide. "Like you, Dad?"

Kenneth felt a lump rise in his throat. "I hope so," he said honestly. "But even more than that, I want you to be better than me. To learn from my mistakes and make choices that reflect the best of who you are."

The conversation lasted late into the evening, with Kenneth sharing stories and lessons from his own life. He talked about the importance of self-respect, of presenting oneself with dignity, and of never underestimating the power of hope and hard work. The boys listened intently, their young faces thoughtful.

As they headed off to bed, Kenneth felt a deep sense of fulfillment. He had planted seeds in their hearts—seeds of wisdom and love that he hoped would guide them through whatever challenges they might face.

Before turning in for the night, Kenneth sat down at his desk one last time. He opened his notebook to a blank page, the final one, and began to write.

"This is the end of one chapter and the beginning of another. Life is a series of choices, and each one shapes the path we walk. I've learned that no matter how far we fall, it's always possible to rise again. To my sons: never stop striving to be the best versions of yourselves. Carry hope in your hearts, and let it guide you toward a life of purpose and meaning. This is my story, but it's also yours. Write it well."

As Kenneth closed the notebook and set it aside, he felt a sense of completion. The man he had become was a far cry from the boy who once sagged his pants, searching for identity in the wrong places. He had found his identity not in rebellion, but in growth—in love, in family, and in the quiet strength of hope.

He turned off the light and climbed into bed, Carla's steady breathing a comforting presence beside him. As sleep claimed him, Kenneth dreamed of a new dawn—a future bright with possibility and the promise of all the seeds he had planted taking root.

www.ingramcontent.com/pod-product-compliance
Lightning Source LLC
Chambersburg PA
CBHW050029040225
21389CB00010B/694
* 9 7 9 8 3 0 1 9 9 6 0 1 6 *